Urmilla Deshpande lives in Tallahassee. Her works include *Slither: Carnal Prose*, *A Pack of Lies*, and *Kashmir Blues*. She is working on her next novel, based on her grandmother, Irawati Karvé. Although Karvé went on to become a respected academic and award-winning writer, the novel is about her time as a PhD student in Weimar, Berlin in the 1920s.

Body and Blood

Stories on Breaking the Ten Commandments

URMILLA DESHPANDE

SPEAKING
TIGER

SPEAKING TIGER PUBLISHING PVT. LTD
4381/4, Ansari Road, Daryaganj
New Delhi 110002

Copyright © Urmilla Deshpande 2019

ISBN: 978-93-88874-43-4
eISBN: 978-93-88874-42-7

10 9 8 7 6 5 4 3 2 1

The moral rights of the author have been asserted.

'Beyond the Pale' was first published in *Slither: Carnal Prose*, by
Tranquebar Press, Westland Books, 2012, and reproduced
here with the permission of the author.

Typeset in Arno Pro by SÜRYA, New Delhi

CONTENTS

i

Body and Blood

I am the Lord your God. You shall have no other
gods before me.

I've tried on everything in my closet. I have decided on the cobalt dress. There is something this colour does to my skin. All other blues are off limits for me, they bring out yellows and greens in my skin in a most unflattering liver disease kind of way. But not this cobalt dress. This is the only dress I have remade every time my body changes. The silk is raw handmade and hand-dyed, I have a bolt of it so I will have this dress as long as I live. I pull the zipper up the side and pull my breasts forward one by one to fit into the tailored corsetted top. It's made so that I don't need to wear a bra. I put on my grandmother's Burmese ruby earrings, and then the bracelet. Thirteen massive bloody squares in a barely visible claw setting make a lovely weight, pulling down slightly like Evy's loose grip around my wrist. I always wear these to church on Sunday, for Holy Communion, when I receive the body and blood of my Lord. Always, because these were given to me at my confirmation, though I was too small to wear them till I was twelve or thirteen.

I almost threw away the card with the rest of the mail. Dull black, I felt the heft of it, my name gently handwritten on the envelope, and so I opened it. I was invited to dinner, date, time, place: Today, 6 pm, Merlin's Passage. The house across from the small but steep valley that divided us from the world on that side. Mine is the only house on the estate from which that house is visible, and I have a small stand of water oaks struggling for survival between my windows and the view, but the house shows through the dark branches and small leaves… It is a beautiful house, dark wood and massive plates of glass, it crouches in tall grass, tries its best to disappear, and mostly succeeds. I only see it because of the light that reflects off its glass walls. By noon I know that the whole family is invited. We all conclude that the owner of the house has finally, after five years of living there, made this gesture of acknowledgement to her closest neighbours.

She is known only as Annapurna. She might be the most sought-after chef in the world. She is surely the

most secretive. Other than her restaurants being among
the best on every continent, her origins, her sexual
preferences, even her gender are endlessly speculated
about. She is a Nepali brothel runaway, secret consort of
the king of Bhutan, Jaffna rebel queen, she has sex with
animals before she cooks them, she is of indiscernible
sex and chooses to be female. She does bring out the
beasts of public imagination, even here where the per
capita eccentric density is high. I assume she lives
here for the same reasons we do—the wilderness, the
proximity to the city of Los Angeles, the isolation. It
is an area very sparsely populated by the crowd-averse
wealthy.

I have seen her, once. On the drive home from Easter
mass two years ago. The driver braked hard to avoid a
cyclist, I glanced up from my magazine. She was in her
car, waiting for her front gate to respond to her voice, or
remote, or whatever technology she used, and obviously
it wasn't opening. She was driving herself, she had the
window of her 2003 Thunderbird rolled down. The
gate did open and immediately the window went up,
but not before I had glimpsed a long, sharp, straight
nose and shockingly long neck. She had her hair under
a tight cap, so my overall impression was of Nefertiti.
Over the week all of us have shared any information
we have gathered about her in our afternoons at the
pool, it isn't much. She seems to be what is called by

the media an intensely private person. Most pictures of her are accidental, blurry, and vague. She wears black, she covers her head with that cap I saw her in, she puts her hand up in front of her face if she senses a camera. Just like me and my own family. Today we all meet, and, hopefully, get to know her. Days of speculation come to an end tonight.

I am excited. Evy would have loved this. Evy. Sister, mother, friend to us all, the very best of us all. Smartest, kindest, tallest. I miss her, I more than miss her. Everyone says, everyone but us, time heals all—all of us and all our wounds. So we wait, and we try to get through each day, as we are getting through this one. We find things to do, together and by ourselves. Evy's body is still with us, but she is gone. We know one day soon we will have to make the decision, let her go. Begin to grieve, begin to live without her. I am not ready. None of us are.

The door shudders from being hammered on, and within seconds, again. It's Michael, of course. The knocking becomes frantic so quickly. He's so impatient. He surely misses Evy the most out of all of us. Our mother died soon after his birth, Evy was the only mum he had. I'm the next in line, so now I'm his mum. But I really don't have Evy's patience or sweetness, or her love for all things. She is strange too, though, our Evy. Strange enough that she was gone from something in her brain, something that shut it off.

'Anne,' through the window. It's pronounced 'Annuh' like Anne in German.

'Michael, I'm coming, two seconds,' but he's already gone around to the kitchen door, and the dogs are stomping and wagging and panting, I can hear their joy against the furniture and on the floor. Now he pounds up the stairs. And then Michael stands at the door of my dressing room right behind me. He looks wonderful in his dark blue suit. I tell him so. He comes over and hugs me and bites my shoulder. We are a bitish family, I think. We all express ourselves with our mouths and teeth. I remember Evy biting Michael's delicious baby bottom until he cried out, and I could see she had the utmost trouble stopping. She left marks on his peach skin. She left marks on everyone. Evy bit her own lips, or wrist, when she was angry. When she grew up and stopped biting the object of her anger, that is. I'd been bitten by Evy more times than I cared to remember—love, anger, just because I smelled nice was reason enough.

'Come on, let's go.' I pick up my gold chainmail purse. I don't need a purse, but my cloves are in it, and my lighter. There is no one at the cars but the two of us, the drivers are waiting. So I light up a clove and inhale deeply, and let out a nice smokeflower in Michael's direction.

'You're not going to taste anything,' he says, 'and it will be a pity, if she cooks our dinner. You think she'll cook our dinner? Herself?'

I haven't even thought about that, silly me, and my excitement rises. The time comes, the doors of the houses open one by one and everyone comes out. Oh we are a handsome family, and beautifully dressed and made up. Each one of us is so different too. Emily is wearing a suit like Michael's, and her long hair is red this year. Flaming red, rubies and cranberries red, and she wears mother's emeralds that granddad brought for her from Colombia, little and large ones clustered together like mutant grapes all round her throat. She is the most beautiful of my sisters. She is my only sister now. I have an urge to squeeze her. I do, as soon as she is close enough, and I clench my jaw tight from the thing I'm feeling. I don't taste her, but I could. She smells of cloves soaked in blood orange.

And soon we are all standing at the door of our neighbour's house. The glass door reflects all of us with a backdrop of Pacific blue sky, and I see what our host will see as she approaches the door. We are birds of paradise, my siblings and their partners and I. Flaming Emily and her dark Savio, pale Michael and his even paler Joseph, our oldest brother James-Sky and sweet Selena hugely pregnant by him, and Rudy, alone without his Evy. Eight of us, only eight, because Evy, darling Evy, lies in a room of her house tied to the steel and plastic things that run her body—she is not dead, but she is gone. I reach for Rudy's hand, and he takes mine and holds it tight. I see he is wearing Evy's rosary wrapped around his wrist, the tiny gold cross pierces his skin. He has done ever since Evy left us. I saw him take it off her neck. That day, her hair shone purple against the silk of her pillow, a pigeon flew across the window, reflected in her eyes, her indigo eyes, but it didn't fly inside her head, she said nothing anymore. I hold Rudy's hand in one of mine, Michael's in the other, and we wait, suspended in the wait. I have always valued the wait. It is a holding, a time and space of doing and not doing, of being and not being, of reflecting and absorbing. Like waiting in line as others in front of me stand before the priest, I know it's coming, the blessing, the host. I wait.

We don't see the person approach the door, it just opens, sliding not swinging, there is no sound. This person is not Annapurna. It is a young woman, a very small woman with black fingernails and tight black cap holding her hair all within it so I don't know what colour it is. She is very pale, with smudgy eyes. She does not smile, in fact, she shows no movement at all on her face, and before any of us says anything she says, 'Come, it's to be in here,' and walks into the empty, dark wide foyer. We don't look at each other, we follow her through.

The room is massive, really massive. Dark walls recede into shadows far from us. A table runs up and down the room, a long, long table, it could seat thirty each side, but it has only eight chairs on one side. It is wood, thick, polished, old-fashioned in a new sort of way. We sit, and wait again, we say nothing. We are drawn into an intentionally serious mood. The room becomes brighter. We see why the room seemed windowless. The glass has adjusted to let in light from the outside. We couldn't see out before and now we can. I am inside the house I have seen so often from the outside, I think. No one speaks, we feel we mustn't.

A wall slides and she is suddenly in the room, standing in front of us all on the side of the table with no chairs. Annapurna. Nefertiti head, tight black cap. I almost laugh, it's only a modified chef's hat, nothing sinister after all. And she looks at each of us in turn and says our names, and then smiles.

'Welcome to my home, and I hope we will be friends after this night.'

All of us mumble polite things, hello, thank you, and so on. And then I notice the huge envelope she holds in her hands, as she puts it on the table.

'I don't want this to be sinister. But now I need you all to be very patient with me. I have something very important to tell you, and to read to you. I need you all to hold the hand of the person next to you, on both sides, and you Rudy, and you Savio, put your other hands on the table.'

For some reason we do as she tells us. We still do not look at each other, we all look straight at this woman in

front of us. She seems to me to tremble a little, I have
a sense of a bird in my hand. A small egret. Like that
time Evy and I walked at the marsh edge and found
one upside down in a tree, shimmering like paper to
get its foot free, but it couldn't. Evy climbed the tree
as high as she could, she shook the branch with her
whole body weight. Shook, shook, shook. Each time
the bird shuddered, hoping. Opened its wings. After a
long time of trying the bird fell down, but it didn't live
for long. Evy took it home, plucked its white feathers
off, and cooked it and ate it. So I think, is Annapurna
the egret that Evy ate, or just a thin bird woman, and
my thoughts stop, because of what she is saying to us
here, my thoughts are so loud and trying so hard to
distract me, showing me dead birds, Evy sawing through
a long white neck, Anne Boleyn, my namesake, long
white neck, sword, I'm trying so hard not to hear, but
I hear anyway.

'Your Evy is gone. She died this morning. They
disconnected her, she is dead now, really dead. I am
going to wait till you all understand what I have just
said, because I cannot go on till each of you gives me a
sign. Raise your hand, or say something when you are
ready for me to go on.'

Silence.

The waiting is over. Evy, suspended between
doing and not doing, being and not being, reflecting

and absorbing, has stopped now. Rudy is the first to move his hand. And then one by one, we all do it, say something, show we understand. None of us asks how it is her, Annapurna, who brings us this knowledge, this finality, and here, in this manner. We wait, because we all know we will know what is to be known.

She opens the envelope, takes out pages. She holds up a paper, a death certificate. She holds up the other paper. It is written by Evy, in her handwriting. It is signed by Evy. Annapurna reads from the other paper, and she is perfect as Evy's messenger.

'My darlings, it is me. Your sister, your wife, one of you. I am gone now. I wanted to be with you, my sisters, my brothers, Rudy, my love, but I didn't get that, my greatest dearest wish. I have loved you all, you know every one of you how I have loved you, and I know you have loved me. I am grateful to have been yours, and proud that you were mine, you beautiful beloved ones. Live well. I know you will not always be happy, but be always aware of each other. Love each other. Love the child who will come soon, love him a little for me too. I know you will do this thing that I ask you to do for me now. Don't walk away, do this last thing for me, my loves. Trust Annapurna, completely, because I did. She will honour me.'

Annapurna stops reading, puts the paper back in the envelope, and looks at us in that way she does, one by one. She says, 'Will you stay, then, and know what your Evy left for you all?'

No one moves. Something is forming in my mind, but I don't know what it is.

'Yes,' I say, because of course I will stay, and so will everyone else.

And then there are murmurs of yes from the others.

'If there is anyone who wishes to leave for any reason, please do so now,' Annapurna says.

'Why should anyone want to leave?' It is Selena, my sweet, clever young sister-in-law. She speaks for us all. We all know this is about Evy. We have an idea. We all knew Evy well, the parts of her life and self that she gave us, that she wanted each of us to know. We know, I know anyway, and if I know each one here knows, that none of us knew all of Evy.

Annapurna is thoughtful, we wait. She is in a place she has never been in before, as are we. We wait. Like coloured birds on a jungle canopy, we wait. We watch her. She is Lophorina, the superb bird of paradise, the one that swivels shock blues in its blackness so swiftly that you think you might have imagined it.

'I loved Evy,' she says. There it is, the shock blue. 'She knew I loved her.' Annapurna looks straight at Rudy, but there is no apology in her eyes or face.

'You know, Rudy, how it is to love her as I did.'

We are seated so we can't see each other's faces, but

I know Rudy, generous, weak, lost without his strong wife-mother, his Evy. I know he is crying, but I don't turn to look.

'I told her I loved her,' Annapurna says, quiet, 'and she understood, and this is how you come to be here, all of you. She knew I would honour her wishes, I would do as she wanted no matter what.' She wipes tears from her cheeks with fists, like a child does.

'We are here to celebrate your Evy, your sister, your wife, your friend, your mother,' she says, softly. 'And my Evy too, who I wanted but could never have, in any way except this one.'

The woman who opened the door for us comes in now, a long tray in her hand, nine glasses of red on it. She comes around to us, gives each of us a glass, and one to Annapurna. She holds it up, slightly for a moment, says nothing, and we all do the same. And then without more words, we all drink. It is stunningly tart, my mouth puckers in upon itself, I am unable to speak anyway.

Another woman comes in with another tray. A pile of large white plates, golden forks, large white napkins. They are set down before us, and I feel my hunger suddenly. The wine has burned a path into my belly, hunger slices up along it. Annapurna leaves, and returns in minutes, small white plates are placed on the larger ones, they contain very small portions. A spiky dark green leaf, a single thin slice of dark red meat.

'Eat,' she says. I roll the leaf around the meat and place it in my mouth. Salt and sweet and sharp of the shiso leaf, a hint of garlic, a perfect, perfect morsel, evolving in my mouth as I chew, as my spit creates complex nuances of colour and texture in my throat, in my nose. I close my eyes because the pleasure is so intense, so simple. I am overcome with, of all feelings, love. And then I understand.

'Evy,' I say, and Annapurna nods, and I hear the intake of their collective breath, of course they know. Because we all know Evy.

'Shall I go on?' Annapurna asks, and we cannot say yes, but we do not say no, not any one of us. The women come in and take away the small white plates. They all go out again, and return with bowls. Steaming bowls, it is a soup this time. I breathe in the steam, it clings to my face and hair. I look into the bowl, move the liquid with my spoon. It is almost gel but not quite, and there are tiny green stars floating in it. They are not stars, it is my eyes, misty, that make it seem so. I take a spoonful to my lips. Anise, pepper, coriander, a consommé of love, of Evy's bones. It will nourish me forever, I think. None of us have so far looked at each other. I have to. I turn to look at Michael. He takes a spoonful.

'Evy,' he says, 'hello, my love.'

He places his spoon on the table and lifts the bowl with both hands and drinks from it, drinks it till it's all gone.

'And, my love, goodbye,' he whispers, but we all hear him.

The silence is broken now, and we begin to talk, we eat, we laugh, the food comes in waves and in small amounts and large, plates, bowls, platters, pates, crackling, ground up thigh, sliced breast, the inside of her arm perhaps, we don't know and don't care. She wanted to be loved, Evy did. Loved, and all of her. Not buried, eaten by creatures of soil who didn't love her, not burned by searing reductive fire, not thrown away like discarded clothing. To her the body and the being was all one. She was a physical thing, her flesh was her. She wants us to love her, and we do. This is not a meal, this is a ritual outpouring of love. Annapurna has honoured her, truly. She has interpreted Evy. Evy is delicious in every single morsel. She is lovingly prepared, and lovingly paired with so many different things from the world she loved, so many leaves, and flowers and birds and berries and fruit and fats and oils. We are replete with Evy, with love of her, and with grief and joy of her, and smell and taste of her—we have consumed Evy, she is within us, she is us, and we are her now.

Finally, Annapurna brings in a chair and sits down in front of us. The plate in front of her is white, Evy's heart sits on it, large, dark, it smells of ghee and whisky, and there is a small puddle of creaminess below it on the plate. Annapurna has a fork, but she hesitates.

'Rudy,' she says, 'I know she was yours, and this is rightfully yours. But—if you say I can—I want it, more than anything.'

'What did she say to you?' Selena asks, because she knows, as we all do, that Rudy will not.

'She said I could, if you all agreed. I wanted what was not mine, and I knew it then, and I know it now.'

We let her have it. She deserves it, right or wrong. We watch her though, as she eats, slowly, thoughtfully, with love. She leaves nothing on the plate. At the end, she puts the fork down and picks up the plate. She holds it up so we can't see her face, and when she puts it down again, there is not even a smear on it. There is a smudge of blood, Evy's blood, on the side of her mouth, and we watch her tongue come and take that away, and a smile of fulfilment appear in its place.

When Evy and I were girls growing up in the family compound in Old Goa like all the generations before us, back then before we did the never-before-done and left the compound and the country, we saw Saint Francis Xavier in the Basilica of Bom Jesus. He was in a glass box, the glass was all fogged on the inside and scummy with finger and face and nose prints on the outside. Evy and I deposited our nose and fingerprints too, before our mother dragged us away from there. Evy was fascinated by someone being in a box. Couldn't stop thinking about it.

'Will we put Nanna in a box too, when she dies?' she asked our mother, and Nanna came up behind us and heard her, and said, laughing, 'Yes, Evy, they'll put me in a box, but they won't display me like Francis Xavier. They'll put me in the ground. Thankfully, because the Lord knows, if the way I look now is any sign of what's to come, I have no desire to be displayed.'

My mother and grandmother became involved in a conversation about funerals, so Evy skipped away and out of the kitchen door, dragging me behind her by the wrist. We spent a lot of time making pastes. Green ones from leaves, magenta and white ones from dead flowers, yellow ones from dead leaves. We spread them over each other's arms and faces and pretended we were goddesses. I liked gods and goddesses. Until, that is, I saw Saint Francis in a box. He was a real body, not just a picture on a wall, or a small golden or silver statue. He didn't have a hundred arms and legs, or an elephant head, and he wasn't bright blue with snakes around his neck. But he was a real body. I didn't really know the difference between saints and gods. Still don't. When we were older and returned to see Saint Francis, Evy told me he had a toe missing.

'Anne darling, can you see?'

'Of course not Evy, it's missing,' I grinned as I said it.

'Yes, precious, I mean can you see that it's missing?'

I nodded.

'It was eaten,' she said, and I was enthralled, as she knew I'd be.

The saint is carried on a platform by six strong men, though the saint himself weighs almost nothing. The procession weaves down the street. Flocks of pigeons fly out of the way and settle further up the street, as it comes upon them, again, again, and finally fly up and watch it all from safe above. People, ribbons and bows, flowers and glitter and dancing, a big writhing snake of songs and lights, coming closer and closer and then into the Basilica where the saint will lie, till the next year. A woman swivels in a black robe that swirls around her revealing blue ruffles, she raises her arms high and the robe floats behind her. She approaches the body of the saint, she swoons, she cries, she sings, she is so full of love and desire for the saint, and she cannot help herself. She eats his toe. She bites it off, she chews it, she swallows it down. She is transported into a kind of heaven on earth. She is carried away by the angry crowd and deposited at the edge of town. But she has the saint within her now.

Evy, I want to be consumed, just like you are, I want to live on, just like you live in us. I want to be loved like you are loved. But perhaps not. Perhaps, you are the only one who deserves to be remembered, and received, in this way. Should I love you this way? Should we? We do, that is all there is to it. Do I love you before Christ?

Before God? We don't take communion, anymore. Not one of us does. You Evy, are the only one now, you, our most beloved.

James-Sky and Selena's new baby comes three months later. We name her Evelyn, after her aunt, who is a part of her, in every way but one. Annapurna brings a little vial she has saved for the baby. And then, Evelyn receives her aunt. Body and blood.

I know she's pleased, my Evy, wherever she is.

ii

End of Days

You shall not take the name of the Lord in vain.

Decay. I inhale its emanations with every breath. The taxi is part of a slow traffic swarm. Neither the tightly shut windows nor the hair-raisingly cold air-conditioning suppress the smell of organic breakdown. The warm mélange I took so much care to concoct, a vanilla and cardamom and almond aura of a fresh baked cake, is dissipating fast and being replaced by this pall of decay. Johar is on his way to our rendezvous, this putrefaction will accost him too, draw out his bile as it does mine. I hate the city now. Friends, lovers, companions—make it bearable. We meet in the safe rooms, little islands floating precariously in the filth of the city, contents of sewers flowing beneath us, ejaculations of factories above. Outside the thin walls, the city, a living creature of rank morality and rancid self-righteousness, waits to devour us. My whole life is a series of leaps from island to island, some no bigger than my own footstep, of barely avoiding falling to my end. It isn't just the real physical filth. There are those notices on all the walls, with small symbols on the four corners. No one else seems to notice the irony, the crushing irony of those symbols from another time and place. The warnings on the notices are dire, immodesty and any public display of it would be severely dealt with. Passive voice, active threats. I have heard rumours that the Chanters break down doors if they suspect someone of something. We all assumed these rooms were safe. Because it was better not to think about it. We didn't always use the rooms for lovemaking. They were places to meet and talk freely, smoke a cigarette, drink a beer, buy and sell and do verboten things, because so many things were forbidden. We lived in verbotenland. I paid a lot for a copy of an American underwear catalogue. A catalogue, not even an actual bra. I was lucky I could do without bras, my breasts were small enough that a scarf tied around my chest would suppress any shadow of a nipple. The fine was small. For some. For me, it was the price of a cigarette. And how did they even see nipples, these foetid beige-coloured mummies, these things that policed us, these slugs sweating inside those uniforms that rendered them genderless and soulless? They stared. That's all they did, stared, all day and all night, looking for a nipple, a kiss, a touch, between lovers, friends, even mothers and children. A hug was not a hug if one of these creatures deemed it not a hug but a public display of immodesty. They lurked, on street corners, in trains, buses, foyers of buildings, to impose fines on a hand held, a kiss goodbye, and occasionally, a grab of breast or trouser bulge. They stared, and they saw what they were trained to see: Pleasure. Touch. Sex. To them, decadence. Corruption. Evil.

I lay with him, Johar, his palms parting my thighs, his mouth leaving a trail of spit from my belly to my mouth, only his moans kept the sounds from outside at bay, for moments. This man, how he touched me, he brushed me, he caressed me. He took his time, and mine. He strolled the beach that was my body, he lay in my waves and let the motion carry him, or let the storms drown him. He did not jump and thrust and ride me to his destination. He never seemed to have any destination but our pleasure. He, only he, kept me concentrated on himself and my own senses. With the others, I often feared that with the slightest tilt, we would slip into the filth. I could hear it sometimes, lapping at our island, as I lay in the fading heat of our passion. Passing cars trail light across these walls, the conversation of dogs diminishes only slightly as it passes through them. These things do not alarm me.

They don't frighten me when I am with Johar. The walls are thin, not just the literal walls, but those that contain our last freedoms—they are thin, and prone to break and tear at any moment. It is not so strange that these safe rooms exist in the poorest part of the city. The morality police don't care about the morality of the poor, it seems, and tend to leave them alone, to stew in their own physical and moral stink. Well, we are not poor, and we are happy to take shelter here, in these rooms, and they—the poor—are happy to take our money, and provide us with small services. We buy the food, tea, cigarettes, massages offered. They guard the doors, they are armed. They need us as much as we need them. Most safe rooms are in the former red light district. Sex is sold no more in the broken heart of this city. That may have been a good thing, if the sex workers had been rehabilitated or sent back home, or given other jobs. But they were simply dumped, disease and all, into the warren of prisons recently built on the outskirts of the city where, centuries before, mangrove swamps set down strange roots and the sea began to doubt itself.

I thought about how we had all failed, and in our cowardice and our desire to pretend all was well, we had allowed ourselves to come to this. They had always known that this city held the key to their power. If this city fell, the rest would be easy. To them, this city was the soul of the evil, the source of the depravation that was spreading through the land. This city, with its temples and cinemas, its nightclubs, its money, its shops and whores and industry, was the fountainhead.

It was a decade and a half ago when I first saw Johar. I was fifteen years old. I have never wondered what compelled me to follow him, to stand beside him in the rain, to sneak under his umbrella at the station, to accept a ride in his car as it slowed to a stop in front of us, and a driver with a black hat opened the door for us. I knew then that he was old enough to be my father, but he really wasn't, he was only about fifteen years older than me. Well, he could have been a father at fifteen, but he was as old then as I am now, and he doesn't seem that much older than me anymore. Back then it felt different. It may have been one of the last years my school had that uniform, and the nuns their losing battle with the length rules. We tried to wear it short, they ripped out hems to cover our adolescent knees. But surely even they hadn't wanted it all to go the way it had. The girls' schools did not have those pinafores anymore. The girls all wore saris, with long-sleeved buttoned shirts instead of blouses. They were beige. At every school. The girls no longer had varying lengths of hair, and certainly didn't sneak their mothers' lipsticks on their birthdays. Their mothers didn't have any lipstick to sneak. It was considered a public display of indecency, and carried a fine. The city had fallen, it had caved in on its own delight in itself. Then the enemy had organized itself. It put up candidates for every seat, and made sure they were elected, by any and all means. And here we were, defeated by our own laziness and confidence in the strength of freedom and pleasure. Ugliness had prevailed.

My fifteen-year reign of pleasure was poised to end too, it was getting harder for women to meet, let alone consort with what was designated the enemy. Johar was above their law, or outside it, because he was not of the religion. Not that I had a religion, but my name put me inside their fence. I could have changed my name, perhaps five years ago, but now that was impossible. I would have to produce papers from five generations ago, and I could not. I could have married Johar five years ago, but that was impossible too now, even if he was willing. It was verboten. Along with all the other lovely things that were verboten, this too was decreed a crime punishable by long imprisonment, and permanent separation of the offending couple. And we all knew what happened in those prisons.

And that was how all this began, for me. A dear friend whose name I dare not say was released after nine weeks in one of those places. She is a small, delicate woman, a cupcake, everything made to smaller proportions. A symphony of pastels, her skin, her eyes, her lips, even her voice. But when I saw her after her release she

could not speak. Her mother, also wordless, took me
to her room, where I had been a million times since we
were both schoolgirls, not yet in our teens. She lay in
her bed staring out of a window, facing away from me.
I touched her arm, I didn't want to startle her in case
she was asleep. She flinched, and turned her face to me,
eyes wide and mouth open in an imitation of a scream.
Nothing came out but a wheeze. When she turned to
me, I jerked my hand away from her, because she was
not my friend, whom I had known almost two decades.
This was not her, surely. It was not the lips, the lower
one split open on one side and the upper swelled so it
wouldn't sit right on its mate, perhaps ever. It wasn't
that the whites of her eyes reflected the peculiar yellow
of her skin. I learned from her mother's spare jagged
words that she had severe jaundice from the water they
forced her to drink in the prison, she said it smelled of
human faeces. It wasn't that my friend had been beaten
and probably raped many times for the time that she was
gone. It was none of those things, and all of them, when
seen with the dead darkness of her eyes, that filled me
with fear and foreboding and an acrid rage and sorrow
for what we had all become. I did not stay long with
her, I went looking for the one person who would help
me understand, or help me cling to possibilities that
we were losing to the reality of what the city was—a
distant memory of a place we once arrogantly said we
came from, that we were once proud to call ours.

Johar was in his office in the embassy. It was a haven of glass and steel where the authorities, including the staring slug mummies in their beige rind, had no jurisdiction. I did not go there often, it would have aroused suspicion. Suspicion was the only kind of arousal they felt in the shrunken thing they called a brain. Actual brainscans showed that the size of the hippocampus in men and women—if you could call them that—who worked in the police force, had shrivelled to less than half the size of a normal person's hippocampus. Some academic from some esoteric liberal North European university did trials and published a much publicized study. The upper echelons of government embraced this horror as an entirely desirable effect, one they would strive to achieve across the population. They were mostly succeeding.

I felt victory for a while, when I saw Johar. His face, a creation of decades of rightful arrogance, was a beacon of hope for us, the wretched and oppressed, the weak, ugly, cowed population of this city, or at least for me, their representative. If I was in fact the representative of the rebels of this city, my rebellion was a poor thing, a selfish little construction of walls of secretiveness tentatively encasing nothing but my own pleasure. The victory was short-lived then, and pointless. I lived this life, but there was no substance to it, hardly any reality. Reality, I thought, would come from a knowledge that life could be lived in the open some day, however distant. A life lived joyfully, without guilt, without fear. I hardly ever even dreamed or wished for it now. I had lost my grip on possibility, on hope, I had slipped into the scum, off the island. It was just an illusion, a life lived for momentary pleasures. We had given up. A cigarette, an orgasm, that's what we spent our energies striving for.

'Hey, hey, hey,' Johar said, when he saw my face, the defeat must have been plain in my eyes. He held me a moment, then sat me gently on the narrow black couch against the wall. He called someone, an employee came with a tray, which he took at the door. He came and sat beside me, made me a cup, tea, said nothing as he stirred several spoonfuls of sugar into it. Sugar. Verboten. Pleasure. He knew I would tell him about whatever it was that was nibbling my soul, whatever thin shreds were left of it. I told him. I didn't say my friend's name even here, where I knew it was safe. I no longer trusted my feelings, my knowledge, none of it was permanent. Feelings were unreliable at the best of times, and the basis of knowledge is changeable in a state such as ours. I leaned my head against his shoulder even as I thought, with some dismay, that he himself may turn, and then turn me in. Surely not. Surely not, because even if it wasn't love we felt for each other, it was something, something important that would stop us from betraying each other.

'I have something to show you,' he said, halting my slowly spiralling thoughts. He walked to his desk. The top was so thin that I didn't think there was space for any storage in it, but there was. He brought a small package to show me. He opened it carefully, as if it would break, or explode if moved. I found out that it was exactly why he opened it the way he did. He was respecting its ability to explode.

'Would you do something?' he asked, and thinking about the answer changed my brain. The hippocampus began to swell, the acidic secretions of revenge and retribution began to etch neon paths through all the dead space that once had been my mind.

'Would you do something big? Something very very big?' he said, so softly I wasn't sure he had said it.

I grinned and said, without any doubt, because doubt had been corroded away, indeed I would.

It was a simple, easy plan. Johar gave me a map. The map showed me the way from my apartment to the nearest hidden manhole. That manhole would let me into the sewers. He had given gave me a small package of the explosive. All I had to do was get there at the same time as two others, because the manhole covers were heavy and impossible for a single person to move by themselves and then drag back shut from below. This took some manoeuvring, but wasn't practically hard to do. I did not know who would be there waiting for me, and if he or she was a threat or an ally. That was the moment of the most raw fear.

A man and a woman, they got there at the same exact time I did. I knew they had been told to be on time, to the second if possible. We all approached each other, and we all knew each of us hoped none of us were hunting the others. I uncovered my head and face first. When I first saw the man, I didn't know he would be my companion for all the rest of the time I had left in the world. He looked too much like me, I thought. By the end of our life together I knew that he was intended for me, everything had been carefully planned, down to that final detail, by someone who knew me, and this man, well, and for a long time. But I get ahead of myself. At the manhole, we told each other our names. Obviously the stronger two, Nabil and I handed our packages to the woman, Cybil, and then together heaved the manhole cover away.

And then I truly entered the filth. Under the city, it was dark. Dark, I could hardly see, I didn't know if others were waiting there and could see us. I didn't know if we were already exposed, already being stalked, hunted. Descent, down the metal bars on the side of the wall, the jump down into wet, there, in the sewers, beneath the city, inside the filth, the smell which I had only sensed before, I was in it. For years I had been afraid of slipping into the filth, and now, here I

was, willingly. Decay. I thought then it would never
leave me. But what I was doing there made it incense
accompanying a religious ritual, and the fumes I had
gagged on when I first got there were a pleasure. There
were people waiting there for us. Men, women, many
much like me, many who had been the lovers of my
love, Johar. How long had he planned this, I wondered,
and how old was he really? I didn't know, and found
that after the first shock of understanding, neither I,
nor the others with me, cared. He had given us hope,
he had given us a way out, he had given us the means.
None of us felt anything but pride, and a wild and lusty
lawlessness run through with righteous immortality. We
might all die. That's where the immortality came from.
The deadly force of evil intention, of murderous evil
intention. We had been wounded, and bled too long,
we were weak, and now we would have our day again.
Possibility was intoxicating.

     I understood something about pleasure. I had never
been so alive, so full of sense, so sensuous as I was those
days, slithering on my belly in other people's waste,
laying charges, covering everything in plastic, covering
myself in shit but protecting those precious packages.
There were hundreds of us. Perhaps thousands, because
the sewers were the other city below the city, as large
as its twin above. I grew accustomed to the smell, the
gloom, to speaking below the murmur of traffic above,

and in the slime and fear and grotesque landscape, I fell
in love. With Nabil, my brother in arms. To kiss there
was an abomination, but kiss we did. And touch, and
grope, and with gloved hands and shrouded bodies, we
attempted physical communion. We smoked cigarettes,
drank clean water from carefully wrapped bottles, we
started something. Something real, a real life, in the
dark, in the fear, in the stench, because it was, in a way,
out in the open, there in the unholy underground.

Days, and another two, and another and another till
they lost boundaries, we worked when it was daytime,
in the dark below. Then we'd crawl up into the dark
above, the city night, into our beds, I was no longer
alone. We were so careful, not only because we had to
be, but because we knew, if we were seen, the kisses
and cigarettes would be gone forever. Johar had warned
us all that we must not, could not be captured by the
enemy. If we were—well, if we were, then I had Nabil.
And he had me. That was what we had been paired up
for—we were each to be our partner's conscience. Their
angel of death. Knowing Nabil would be the one gave
me peace, I knew he would not let me down. I wasn't
so sure of myself, I wasn't sure at all that I could do the
same for him.

As we did what we did, they never came to me, these
feelings that come to me as I tell the story. Those beige
things, they hurt us, took our pleasures, our dreams, our

lives and loves, and in return gave us a sickness, a silence in which most of us had existed most of our lives. But they were humans of a kind, they were bodies, much like ours, though untouched and unloved and unfeeling and sense-dead. And in those few weeks, we were doing the practical things that would bring about their end. They would shatter, or they would slip apart into pieces of flesh, whichever way, they would end. Then they would decompose on the sidewalks, mingle with the concrete of fallen buildings. I did not feel for them, then, when I was working to bring them Armageddon. Now I think about it, was I so different then, from them? I was unfeeling and coldly intentional, I was wicked. I was wicked, and there is no forgiveness for me. I could have been forgiven for what I did, but not, I think, for not feeling anything then, for not even considering for a moment that those were people, the ones who would die. The ones I would kill.

The scene was set, then, and the day came, we watched the sun rise together, Nabil and I. We went down to the sewers one last time, one last time in our lives, to make certain our work would come to blood. As we pushed away the heavy iron cover, I looked once more at the engraving of entwined leaves on the metal surrounding sinuous numbers stating the year it was made, ten decades before, and the name of our once fair, and soon to be fair again, city. I wondered if that metal disc would be intact when the sun rose again. We descended those metal bars again, into what I had once, but no more, thought of as the literal hell below us. It was now the place where I had found purpose, and hope, and even love of a kind. There were only a few of us, the core group, checking the wiring. We walked up and down every section of the charges, we made certain the sewage had not slipped past the barriers of burlap and plastic and burlap again. Hours later, when we were certain we would not be defeated in our enterprise by our own secretions and waste, we came out again. It occurred to me that the roaches and rats and other large and dark creatures I knew were down there because I had heard or felt them moving, because I had seen their eyes shine in the gloom, were relieved to see us all go. They would all die, I thought then, and a liquid regret flooded me as bilious revenge so recently had, but there was nothing to be done, and nothing to be gained by dwelling on the thought, and I let it go.

Nabil and I made our way across the wreck of some abandoned building, we walked fast but carefully because the terrain was strewn with dangers to our flesh—giant icicles of plate glass, twisted steel that once held up the building, concrete rocks. I imagined they all longed for the soft touch of the arch of my foot, the fluids of my inner arm. I had known all along, that I would never see Johar again. He had instructed us not to return to the embassy, not to attempt to connect with him or contact him in anyway, and I had not, though I had wanted to. But it hit me, the knowledge I had pushed away, the certainty that he was long gone, as we crossed that patch of urban ground to get to our beds, that day before the day after, the day before Kingdom Come. Thousands would disappear, our city would ignite, civil war would come to the country, neither of us would likely be alive to see what our deeds would accomplish, and all I cared about at that moment was that Johar, the only man I had loved, the only man who had loved me, was gone. I stopped, I held the hand that was holding mine, I closed my eyes against the distant city neon, I let the sadness run through my heart and soul, I let it flow through my eyes, it was over and under and everywhere, it was me. I stopped there in the urban graveyard to say goodbye to him, who had nurtured me all those years of my childhood and my youth, who had nourished my passions so they would not die under the cold hard boot of my cold hard country.

Maybe it was a way to turn away from what I knew I had done, what I had been a part of. I could taste the sewer sludge and dynamite that ran in my veins now, I could hear the end of my life, my bed, my other pair of shoes, my ring, the only adornment I owned, a gift from Johar for the day I became eighteen, a snake eating its tail forever around my finger, the everlasting secrets about to end, their guts exposed to the world like the insides of these buildings that surrounded and housed us. It was time then.

Nabil and I looked into the shocked sky as the world collapsed around us in fire and the streets turned into hell, we stood, still holding hands, there in that small square of earth, and the words left my mouth because I couldn't help them, because when else could I have said them but then and there, at the end of my love, at the end of my life.

'Holy fucking hell, goddamn,' I said, and it wasn't Johar, but I thought it was, who replied, incredibly, with a laugh in his throat.

'You take the name of your Lord in vain,' he said.

iii

Sunday Snow Job

Remember the Sabbath day, to keep it holy. Six days you shall labour and do all your work, but the seventh day is the Sabbath of the Lord your God. In it you shall do no work.

Canada in the winter. Bleak, and awesome in its ability to inspire gloom and awe in my whole entire being. The winter forced me to look for other colour because it leached all the known, familiar colour away. Very soon, what seemed like an expanse of white revealed shades I had forgotten in the chromatic opulence of my home. As the greens and yellows and reds disappeared, I discovered milk white and ash white and sky white. And then cow's milk white and goat's milk white and cigarette ash white and ashblond white and blue sky white and sunset sky white. There were mauves and beiges and peaches and hints of pink in banks of snow, and a whole alphabet of browns in greenless trees. North of Lake Ontario is as far north as I have ever been, anywhere in the world. It is early in the winter, it's only my fourth Canadian winter, and I know that it's early enough that the shimmer and glow and majesty which inspires me now hasn't yet given way to numbness. There was only one winter I had felt that way, and that had not anything to do with the winter. It was me.

The year had started out so well. I had a job, so I didn't have to go back home yet, I had no car, but I didn't mind walking everywhere, it was a friendly city, unlike in Mumbai, where I'd get my ass grabbed, or even my breast, in the middle of crowded Shivaji Park, in the middle of the freaking day. The one thing that defeats all us Canadiennes, even those who have lived here all their lives, is the wind. It makes weather people say 'It is x degrees, feels like minus 19x degrees.' Windchill. The wicked wind. It will take the cold still air and force it through my red wool overcoat, my black wool men's scarf, my purple sweater, my long-sleeved red cashmere T-shirt, my long-sleeved cotton undershirt, my bra, my skin, my blood, muscle, fat, to my bone. And from there it radiates outwards and freezes me from the bones out.

So I stood in the late morning darkness with my back to the wind, waiting for it to pause for a moment so I could run across the road to the diner, an amber firelit cave with soup and bread and maybe poutine, food of the gods. And maybe someone would like the look of me and I'd make the week's rent. I stamped my feet. The white dislodged from the black suede over-the-knee boots I had spent three nights' takings on. They were worth it. Canadiennes, waterproof and snowproof. My soul was chilled, but my feet were warm. And then this man came striding down the sidewalk towards me, arms outstretched, and he said, 'Today is the day of the hug, and you are the first person I have seen, please hug me.' I didn't think about it. He was tall and broad enough to save me from the wind and cold for the few moments it takes to hug someone, so I tucked myself into his long black winter coat, put my arms around him so my hands met each other against his warm back, and I stood there, my shivers dying in little quakes as I listened to his heartbeat. His heart beat. Snowflakes popped up in the air around us, danced in the patterns of the wind. I smelled him and heard him. How long we stood there I don't remember or care, but in that time he found me out. Not what I did to pay my rent and college tuition, but everything else. Everything that was important anyway.

'Some food? You would like a dinner?' he asked me. I heard his voice through his chest. I knew at once he was not from here, he had a funny accent, but not funny like mine. Different funny. I understood him perfectly, but his words did not follow a familiar ordering or cadence. It was fun to listen to him, so I said yes. And yes, I was hungry, very hungry. His accent gave me visions of a bourguignon, a glass of red wine, hot hard porous bread. And poutine. I really wanted the poutine. It would warm my mouth and hands and marrow. I could probably afford a coffee at Tim Horton's. I wasn't ready to come out of the big hug yet, though. I had created a small nest of my own scarf and hat for my face, warmed by his warmth and my own breath. My adult parts felt silly, a little nervous, but my child part was happy and warm and forgot the cold-blooded moon, the warnings about strangers, and I was clutching on to his long golden locks, angels' voices whispered to me. Yes, I was hearing a familiar voice, and I was brave enough for the changing of the guards. The longer I stood there, the harder it was for me to step away, the harder it was to go back to the life I knew before this hug. The year had started well, yes, but by the day of the hug, it was at the lower end of a downward slide. Not a spiral, just a fall. I had a student visa, so going home was not yet an issue, but paying the fees was. I didn't have the support of a parent, and certainly not of a husband, though his parents did send me some money on and off, when they remembered, they were rather old. I wondered often if I should call and find out if his life insurance paid off. I would at least not have to worry about tuition then, or take money from lonely men for what were really just acts of willpower. But by the moment of the hug, my confidence, my boyfriend, my best friend, were lost to me. Though I was quite happy to continue being her best friend even if she was my ex-boyfriend's new girlfriend. New squeeze, he was a bit of a squeezer. It had been fun, with him. I hadn't known sex could be fun, till I went to bed with him. No, it was the back seat of a car, not a bed. It was a big car, he drove a limo for a taxi company. They paid him enough to cover the rent, but it meant he was bleary and sleepy during classes and labs, and I covered for him a lot. I'd cover for him, even now, if only he, and my ex-best friend, would get over themselves and pay attention to the fact that I wasn't that troubled by their attention to each other, but would have liked to keep them, or at least her, as my friends. They would get over their embarrassment someday soon, I suppose, and their guilt over their betrayal of me and so forth. I didn't care that much. They didn't get it. They assumed that the fact that I had walked in on them was unbearable to me. It really wasn't. They had been kissing, his hand was deep in her bra, and he wasn't able to extricate it before I walked right in. I really didn't care, and I tried to tell them, but they weren't listening. I tried to tell them that I had walked in on my late husband too, I had that universally unforgettable image imprinted on my memory. But I had managed to blur it, mostly. If I made the effort, I could still sharpen it. Easily, actually, it didn't take much effort. I could remember the half-dressed woman, or should I say half-undressed—they must have been frantic for penetration, and she just hadn't managed to take all her clothes off. Either that, or they had been fucking all day and were doing it one last time before they got their pants back on. Before I came home. In any case, I remember the exact shade of orange of her silk blouse, it's a shade I can never wear, or never will. I remember her dark curly black hair, and most of all I remember her fingers. Her legs were apart, she had very black hair, she had one hand holding the flesh apart with two fingers, and the other rubbing what must have been her clitoris. I couldn't quite see it, but I imagine that's what she was rubbing. My husband's dick was pumping into her, he was standing up. I had this amazing view of the whole scene because they were in the TV room, which was in our basement, and I was standing at the top of the stairs looking down. So there it was. An obviously stunning-looking woman, her skin was an unpolished copper and her hair black and curly, and she said something in a voice that made my hair stand on end, words I did not understand, my husband of fifteen years, trying very hard, and I mean hard, to bring her to a quick orgasm. I didn't say a word. I waited, they strained, he came, she told him to stay still while she worked, until, after a quiet, breathtaking shudder, she stopped. Beautiful fingers. They didn't speak to each other as she put her remaining clothes back on. I went back upstairs and to my car. I waited, with my head ducked down, till she came out and drove off. I went back in the house and told him I'd seen them. He apologized, cried, said it meant nothing and so forth. I forgave him, we lay in our bed all night saying nothing and not making contact. He woke up and drove to work the next morning, didn't make it, died in a crash. Early morning drunk driver, killed four people including my husband, and survived.

So, this was neither a surprise nor particularly unpleasant for me, walking in on my two friends. I told myself I was relieved, and then found I really was relieved. I found it hard to bounce the bed every night. It was fun at first, but I didn't like the idea of sex as my cardio for the day, every day, with no break. And I didn't like that it was just that—cardio for the day. Fun. We were friends, but that friendship didn't come with us into bed. It was hung up at the door, and picked up again in the morning on our way to school. I hadn't liked sex with my husband. I didn't like sex with my boyfriend. I was at the point where I was becoming convinced that I just didn't like sex. Of course my job was not sex, I don't consider it sex unless it's recreational, or friendly, not when it ends in an orgasm for one person and cash for the other.

The hug. My thoughts ceased being coherent, being about my own life, and began to take on a bits and pieces quality. A child cuts a finger visciously deep, and it is healed in days. Then there is the scab, to pick. And perhaps, if it is still soft in the centre, to make bleed again. A sense of gasoline from the car in front, at a red light. Transient, the red and the whiff. The steering wheel, warm from the sun on cold hands. A sense of falling, from the sound of the church choir. A stretch inside a warm duvet, a rearrangement of two bodies in disarray from night moves, to fit together neatly, mouth on neck, arm between one breast and the other, knees, all four, in a pile like perfectly folded laundry, a little more sleep, a sleep between two people, a man and a woman, but it could be any two people, if they only would. He does not have a walking stick yet, but he will. Finding that lost tune, at the red light. Maybe this time it will stay, and can be recalled at will. Maybe. And then there are images and ideas, they bring tears or choking and it's all wrong, too sentimental, kitsch, crap, you really don't want it to affect you and still it does. And you shake it off with a bit of self-contempt. And turn away to hide your just-like-everyone-else-ness, and vow to be more careful next time, not let heart overtake mind, not let who you are overtake who you want to be. Who do you want to be? The woman in the car, the one with the cigarette that doesn't sour her breath or maul her lung cells over the edge to a cancer that will kill her? Just a cool smoker, kissed by angels. The one who looks good in Janis Joplin's coat which she bought at a thrift store in LA, she doesn't even know who Janis is. She blows her hair away from her eyes with her lower lip, she narrows her eyes a little, and the creases around her eyes are beautiful, not those redneck smoker creases, she isn't even white. She probably has the same job that I do, she slows down and a man gets quickly in her car. There is a transactional quality to the event that I recognize.

It was warm. I forgot what cold was, inside that hug. The strangeness of it lingered, but became background noise in a little while. And then the strangeness disappeared, and I got used to it. The warmth, of course, I was grateful for that, and then within seconds of our togetherness I got used to the smell and feel of a man whose face I hadn't seen for more than a minute, I couldn't pick him up in a line-up if I had to. He had a wool hat and a scarf covered his mouth and chin. If I could assume hug position with each guy in the line-up, then I could pick out mine. I would know his smell, a wisp of smoke, dregs of coffee and smear of bacon fat, a little vanilla at the edges, where the crumbs of a cake had stuck. I would know the slow beats from his chest, punctuated by a kind of muted huff, and the deep, full breaths. And I would know this hug, the way he had both arms in a protective loop, and one hand on my head, blocking out the sounds of the world so I could disappear into his veins and arteries and chambers of his heart. I was getting lost inside. I was suddenly afraid I would vanish and never be heard of again. At that moment when the panic started to build, he let go. Gently, so I wouldn't fall or freeze, and he stepped back.

'Thank you. A hug, you know, very important. So many days since I touched another person, I was getting weak, and angry. And then I saw, day of the hug, so I come out, in this, for a hug.' He gestured at the cold and wind. He had a funny face. I don't mean funny to laugh at, I mean full of fun. He had seen lots of funny things, or found lots of things funny, something like that. His face had been used for laughing and smiling, a lot. And he didn't have golden locks, just dark hair, under the wool cap. 'So. I buy you a lunch, for this nice hug?' I hadn't seen his mouth yet, it was inside the scarf.

I said yes, and pointed at the diner I was headed to before the hug. We crossed the road. He seemed a little bit older than me, but I couldn't tell. Inside, warm, nice lights, booth tables, the definition of cosy, we peeled off clothing and made a mound of it. I slid around the mound to the window, and he sat across from me. I could see him now, the man I had hugged. And something odd happened to me.

No, I'm not usually like that. But, like a food you

haven't tasted yet draws you to put a morsel in your mouth by inciting your imagination just by the way it enters your eyes, something about him, everything about him, went straight to my orality. Your mouth knows, or imagines the flavour that will flood your tongue and the resistance your teeth will meet when you chew it, so you pick up the food, you take a bite, and whether that simulation was accurate or incorrect, you forget what you imagined and concentrate on what you get. And that was how it was with him. My desire was there, in my mouth. I was hungry and thirsty for him. I think it began with his smell, and now I wanted more. His perfume, his bitterness and sweetness and salt and sour, I wanted to inhale and chew and swallow him. No, I'm not usually, or ever like that. I smoke cigarettes, I bite my nails, I chew gum, I often pull at my mouth or play with my lips. I am oral, yes. But I am not that way in bed. I am normal, really. I kiss, I sigh a bit, I assume the usual positions, I have self-induced more orgasms than with any partner, but I don't make too much of a fuss about that either way. It was never that important to me anyway, either to make it happen, or to inform the man, and it was usually a man, that I was not done yet. Normal, moderately sexual, easily distracted by birds outside the window, or the flowers on a pillow, or the asymmetry of breasts in a painting, to make it to orgasm too often. Never when I was working, but, as I said, I didn't equate that with sex. That was work. Normal, that is, until I met him. And there, in the small booth of a Canadian diner, snow outside, warm inside, hugged and hungry, as I said, I didn't care about sex very much, this was something else entirely. We did not say anything about sex, of course, as I thought my thoughts and drooled my drool. I wanted to stuff my face with him. His mouth, his ears, his fingers and toes, and of course, yes, all that. But we spoke about the menu, diners, the snow, the wind, socialized healthcare, the recession, the American election, the stupidity of mothers' days and hug days and groundhog days. Strange. I began to think about what to do next.

'A soup?' he asked me, and I remembered that was what I had wanted in the first place, and he had paused me in my quest for just that. Soup it would be. As he ate, and talked, I did a frantic mental stroll through my apartment to check if it was in reasonable enough nick to invite him over. Because if I didn't, I knew that this was it, after this meal, this hug, he would be gone, forever. I imagined my life after, every day and every hug and the smell of every man thereafter turning into a variety of sawdust. Time sawdust, touch sawdust, flesh sawdust. I would kill myself one day in that future sawdust wasteland, if I didn't take him home today.

'My wife works every Sunday,' he said, and my stomach went sour and all the heat so carefully constructed by my layers of clothing and soup and the diner heating and of course his hug, began to dissipate through my eyes. I didn't catch what he said after that. I stared into the soup, pushing the pieces of meat from side to side. It congealed, as did I. My day of killing myself was to be sooner than I thought. Killed by a hug.

'Hello? Is the soup so bad? Or was my question too bold? I apologize, really.'

'What?' I said, the slightest hope floated in the air in front of my face. It was probably steam from his cocoa, the waitress had just put it down in front of him.

'I said, are you okay? Did my question upset you?' he said, and I asked, quite steamy now, 'What question?'

'Would you like to come home with me?'

I stood up and began to put clothes on from the heap next to me, thinking I'd be peeling them off again soon. Heat returned to me, it seemed to be emanating from my thighs. He laughed.

'Yes? You would? Or are you leaving?'

I was, honestly, confused. The cold, the hug, the soup, my thoughts were a flurry of snowflakes falling and floating on the wind that was his presence. I knew we would be in his room soon, naked, and that thought almost choked me with icy excitement, I knew I would be naked, and he would be naked, my imagination failed and my heart began to pound. How had this want deserted me for so long, I thought, it had frozen hard in successive winters, those nights when I had stood on street corners or inside bars and cafés, student whore waiting for a man, it had congealed like bacon fat and was now beginning to soften and emanate a warm pig smell.

He stood up too, towering over me. He had mentioned a wife. I actually giggled when I imagined her turning her key in the lock, walking into their house, or apartment, walking into their bedroom, she would make eye contact with him, because I would have my back to her, I would never know, as he groaned and I swallowed, as his big hands full of my hair tightened my scalp and let go again, I would not even know she had been there until I heard the door slam behind her.

I was confused, because I wanted to go home with him, and do whatever came to us to do. And I was confused because I knew he knew, and he was taking me home because he knew. And I was going anyway. The waitress, she smiled at me and touched her cross. I left her a tenner. It was Sunday morning. We were working girls, Sunday or no Sunday. I could have refused the money. I didn't. Sunday or no Sunday, there was rent. There was tuition. And he pleased me. And he paid me more than I have ever been paid.

The priest would hear about my latest sin next Sunday, his young voice old with repetition. I thought of his sadness that very morning, when I recounted and begged forgiveness, which he granted of course, no matter what I said. He'd be hearing this one every Sunday from now on. I had found my first regular, hadn't I?

iv

Honour. Or Not

Honour your father and mother.

Cobwebs trailed frail elegant circles as the fan made slow rotations over me. A laugh and a scream, both rose at once, and stuck, filling my throat, and I couldn't dislodge either. I was in shock, or aftershock. The skyscraper of trauma I lived in was vibrating. I thought, this could be me on the top floor, this moment could be the pointy spire on the very top, and I'd soon be able to see forever. Or maybe, I was at floor level, and this moment was the door to the building, the one by which I would leave. I felt the air move, I watched the cobwebs, like streamers on a maypole, I felt the body on top of mine rise up with my chest on every inbreath. Gravity settled it back on me, pushing out my breath, again and again. I recognized the hardness of my twenty-two carat

gold crucifix gouging breast tissue, it was the only thing
of my mother's that I still had. I was alive, and breathing,
repeatedly, and strongly, that body atop me heaving up
and down because I was.

Death is always near us. We ignore it, constantly and
continuously, just like we breathe. Both keep us alive,
the ignoring and the breathing. We turn away from it,
death, constantly and continuously. It's the opposite
of a scratch in the eye that always, always, skips just
out of vision—death, always, always threatens to come
into view, and we continuously adjust so we don't see
it. As normal as breathing. We pretend it doesn't exist,
so we can allow ourselves to fall asleep at night, so we
can wake up each day and do things, make things, feel
things, pretend that we are different, and apart from,
the couch, the cat, the person who lays on top of us,
dead. In moments like these, like a light switched on
in a gloomy room, the hideous colours of the walls
are revealed, and we always knew they were there all
the time, death is with us all the time. Like paint, or a
soundtrack, to each life, and all lives.

As I lay there with this revelation, Charles
Cardoza popped into my head. Cheerful and quiet,
understanding and sympathetic, dealing every day with
death and the dead. Dealing with death in a way we
never do, and because of that, he always had the light
switched on in his room, CC did. He lived with it, he

didn't try to hide from it, or suppress its presence, he knew its omnipotence in his, in all our lives. The colour on the walls of his room was no longer hideous to him, he had got used to it, accepted it, and eventually, he embraced it, honoured it, he didn't fear it at all. Well, I didn't know that for sure. But, I thought, this—my—situation wouldn't terrify him like it did me. He was a caricature of a mortician. Always the dark suit, dark comb scrapings through greased neatly parted hair, and surprisingly, always a gentle smile. That's what I thought when I first saw him. I met him when Penny's grandfather had died, at the funeral home. He asked Penny what she wanted done, how she wanted her beloved and only living relative, now dead, to look the last time she would see him. We were thirteen then, Penny and I, and CC must have been in his late teens or early twenties. His family had owned that Byculla funeral home for generations. It was once the only one in our dark corner of the city, probably only one was enough in those days, when the Catholic community was much smaller than it is now. Penny had seen her parents, her three aunts, her two brothers, and finally, her grandfather, embalmed and displayed in open caskets in this funeral home, and it seemed like routine for her. CC, however, for whom all this was certainly much more routine than it was for Penny, never let that show, never let it be seen that for him this was just another body to be drained of its fluids, pumped with other fluids, propped up from inside and out in small and large ways, dressed, made up, posed, made ready for its final close-up. He was so loving to Penny, so courteous. He asked her all his questions with the best possible words for the occasion. He asked what Penny's grandfather's favourite suit was, not which one fit him, for example, because Penny's grandfather had been, was, enormously fat. I saw that he had cut the old man's always disgusting fingernails, and remembered a song from the musical *Oklahoma*, about poor Judd who lay dead, and how his fingernails had never been so clean. A loving and caring mortician, like CC, I had thought. And I wondered even then, before I knew him as well as I do now, if it wasn't the honour and love he felt for death itself that made him act the way he did. If he treated bodies with respect because they belonged to his muse, to death now. He fascinated me. He wasn't someone who stood out, he wasn't someone anyone but me really noticed. Everyone in the community had dealt with him or met him, at least all the regulars at our church had. But no one really noticed him as I did. Even Penny wasn't able to answer all the questions I asked her about him on the way back home. Was he young or old, I had asked her, and did he go to school, or did he just grow up and become educated there, in the funeral parlour? Did he live there? I was so fascinated,

I have to admit, that I didn't even know what questions to ask her. She had no answers for me anyway, she was heartsick and incoherent from the loss. Somehow, her grandfather's death had brought back the grief of every other death in her small life like an allergic reaction to a bedbug bite that inflames every bedbug bite you've ever had in your life. I had to put my intense interest in CC aside and console my dear friend. I had to do more than that, she was alone in the world, and we had to find a way for her to live.

How was I to know, at thirteen, that my obvious, generous idea would put my beloved friend on the final steps of her own life? How was I to know? If it had been a bit later, if the things that happened to us after she moved in had already begun to happen to me, I would never have brought her into my house. I didn't know. I thought, she's lost everyone she had who was family, I had one person left who was family to me, why not share my joy? I didn't know, there was no joy to be had there, and I shared only misery with her, and brutality, and as a result, mine was halved, it was true.

I remember the first day we realized we were in hell. Together. We were giggling like schoolgirls, because that's what we were, schoolgirls, in the dark, just like we did each night right before we went to sleep. We both shut our eyes and mouths and feigned sleep when a thin snake of light came in through the opening door, sneaked across the floor and under my bed. What happened after that happened each and every night, either to her or to me. It began with me though, and for sure, I'd rather be skinned and rolled in salt than go through that first time again, and I'm sure Penny would choose that too, but she died and brought an end to her family, and skinning and salting was no longer a choice. My father dragged me by my arm out of my bed and across the hall and down the stairs and into his bed. I didn't resist that time, that first time, because I didn't know what was to come. He was a big man, big enough to flatten me with his weight as he was doing now, but then, before I knew what all that was, I was confused. There's nothing to tell in any relevant detail that would make mine, and poor Penny's, experience different from any other female children who are raped by a close adult relative repeatedly and for a long period of time. Nothing to see here, move along then.

Penny, though, her story was different. Whether it was all that death and loss in her life that made her cling to the only adult presented to her, or whether she genuinely, though in the most twisted way possible, loved this man, I will never know. But Penny, once my friend, couldn't bear that I shared her beloved's bed every other day. Penny, I would rather have been skinned and rolled in salt, you didn't have to die over this. But Penny didn't understand the rape, the facts, the horror of what was happening to her, to us, and, literally insane with grief, rage, jealousy at what occurred between me and him, she threw herself off a ledge high enough that death was with her when she landed. If I had known to be quiet, if I could have lied about it, if I had understood, I would have done something. But I did not. I knew she stood outside the door every other night when I was the one on that bed, but I didn't know why. I thought it was a kind of support for me, once her dearest friend, I thought she wanted to let me know she was there, in spirit, helping me get through it. I was not a screamer, not really, but there were times when I couldn't help myself, when he turned me over the wrong way, when he brought things to hurt me with, when it wasn't just the bearable clutching and thrusting. I didn't understand that those were not sounds of her friend's pain and misery, but rather, my screams and groans pierced her heart, they were manifestations of what should never happen, of her lover, her beloved, her, her, her *man* loving someone else. Poor Penny. She didn't understand that there was nothing but hatred and violence in that house. Poor Penny, poor, stupid Penny, poor stupid dead Penny. Dead, and broken.

That was when I saw CC again. We went to the funeral parlour, my father and I, and there was no one left to say goodbye to Penny except him and I. CC was busy, the secretary told us it would be a few minutes.

Then he came out, and, when he saw us there, he nodded at me perfunctorily, and took my father's hand in both of his, and seemed unwilling to let go. He gazed at him adoringly the whole time we were there, much to my disgust. CC touched his arm when he spoke, I saw him brush his fingertips down the huge arm along the cloth of the sleeve down to the back of the hand, and then draw back as if he had received a shock when his fingertips encountered skin. I looked at my father and saw the brute that left bruises on my body, inside and out, I saw the bear strength that held me down easily, with one hand, one arm. I heard the growl of his contemptuous laugh if I ever resisted, something I rarely did anymore. I saw the ugly cruel mouth, heavy, sneering, where the contemptuous laugh found its way out of his muscular, violent body. CC didn't see him as I did, obviously. He saw what everyone but I saw. He saw what Penny must have seen, I suppose. An enormous god of a man, dark eyes under perfectly shaped brows, thick dark hair flowing straight back from a narrow but smooth forehead, a massive, clean jawline with the faintest shadow. An impressive hulk of a man. Who was impatient, and told CC he had no time to wait. He had instructed me to stay and figure out Penny's funeral arrangements, and then lifted his muscular bulk out of the chair, and left the room. I saw CC's eyes on him till he was gone, and CC must have seen the huge backs of his thighs in the dark pants, the movement of his behind. I had seen this monster naked, I had seen this thing, naked and erect, sneering and ready to crush me, every other night. I remember thinking at that moment that it would now be every night, now that poor stupid Penny had taken herself out of the equation.

CC told me he would soon be back, and I was to wait for him. There was something oddly urgent about the way he left, and I, without thinking, got up and followed him. He went along the corridor and turned left into a doorway. I waited a second to make sure no one would see me, and went in after him, and almost fell down a flight of stairs. Double doors with glass windows in the top opened when I pushed, and I went in. It was cold there, very cold, and minimally lit. I was quiet, and tiptoed, along the corridor. The first door opened into a small room and I almost screamed, but held it down to a gasp. There was a body on a low table, a chair was pulled up next to it. There was no one there. I moved to the next door, and pushed it open very gently. It made not a sound. The set-up was the same, another body, this one face down, but here was CC, slowly drawing down the sheet that covered it, stroking it with his other hand. He dropped the sheet to the floor and pushed the legs apart, and I saw it was probably a man. The legs moved apart without any resistance, without any life. Well, of course they did, but it was still something

I noticed. And then I saw CC had stopped stroking the body and was stroking himself. He had his back to me, but I knew perfectly well what he was doing. I had seen my father do it, when I was bleeding. He made me do it sometimes. There was a sound from behind me and I flattened myself against the wall. I waited, afraid someone would come, but there was no one. A few minutes just to make sure, and then I unstuck myself from the wall and turned back to look at CC. He had climbed onto the body, he was really doing what I thought was not possible, surely, to do to a body that was—that was—well, dead. But he was doing it. Of all the things I could think, I thought, well, at least he's not hurting anyone. That body was not a person, it could feel no pain, it could feel no humiliation, it could never be scarred for life, it was past all that. And I thought no less of CC after all. If anything, he fascinated me all the more.

The cobwebs caught my attention again, and I realized I was doing it again, ignoring, attempting to ignore death when it was spectacularly, heavily, literally on top of me. Not mine, no, but certainly this man was dead, on top of me. I had to acknowledge it, I couldn't just lie here below him, he wasn't going to heave his sweaty bulk off of me by himself, I'd be doing it for him this time. I had a small moment of victory in knowing that, of all the hundreds of times he had mauled my thighs and bitten my shoulders and inserted the pre-greased instrument of pleasure, or torture, or who knows what, into my always paper-dry body, this time, he got no pleasure from it. Death was on my side this time, and took him before he was ready, before he was done. He would never again be done, and, before the scream or the laugh, an intense, surreal, physical pleasure, glowed up and down my whole squashed body. Once I got his body off me, once I got out from under this dead weight, I would never be under it again. Never. Why had I thought of CC, I wondered, as I shoved the thing that was left of my father, my tormentor for seven years, off me. He fell hard off me and off the bed, landing face up on the floor. I worried for a moment that his head could have been injured, and that made me laugh. And scream. The laughter dislodged first, in dry, and then slobbery, spitty yelps, and finally, the scream, I turned my face down into the pillow and smothered it, and it too seemed endless. I had to stop to breathe, and I didn't let it start up again even though I could have, after that deep and shuddering lungful of pillowair. I looked down at him, and I knew why I had thought of CC, and of his almost desperate desire to touch this thing when it was a person. I hoped he would.

We sat outside the funeral home on a cement bench under a very broad tree. It had been shedding leaves all that day, probably all that week. They were thick underfoot, a mattress under the bench. The last one to fall the brightest yellow. I imagined the cross-section of the earth below us darken and darken deep below us. The sky was heavy and low, and I felt sandwiched between the dark above and the dark below, but my spirit was not dark, nor heavy. I felt light as cobwebs released from fan blades, leaves shaken free from trees, free-floating. Everything comes down, everything turns dark, sure. But not yet. I was illuminated, free.

I sat quietly and listened to CC. He told me about his morning, for some reason, because I had told him about mine. I had told him all of it. All. From our beginning, when we had met, at the funeral of Penny's grandfather, to right now. I had left nothing out. I told him what had happened to Penny and why she had died—why she had killed herself. And I told him what I had seen him do that day, the day Penny had died. And he had been so stunned and silenced and rooted to the spot with shock, and maybe curiosity, that he couldn't get up and walk away. I had put my hand on his before I told him, and I had held it hard in case he tried to leave, but he did not. I felt him flinch when I said, 'I followed you, down to the freezers,' and I prepared to prevent his departure. I didn't dwell on what I saw, I wanted to tell him that I didn't judge him adversely, in fact I didn't think his preference, or choice, to commune with unliving flesh, was in any way abhorrent to me.

I told him that it was nothing, his act, or acts, if that wasn't the only time, compared to what had been done to me, and to Penny. We could feel, were made to feel, things we never wanted. He was a good man, I said, for not doing that, for not forcing himself on others less powerful, who didn't want what he wanted. I began to believe what I was saying as I said it, I began almost to admire the man next to me, for finding pleasure in the newly dead. I think I still believe that, feel that. That if, in fact, what CC does is a perversion, it is so harmless that it should be allowed. Encouraged, even.

And then we sat in silence for a while, me still holding his hand. He began to speak to me, and from all he said, I know now that he believed me, that I did not find him repulsive or abhorrent. I was sitting there after all, holding his hand, in spite of knowing what I did about him.

'It started a few years ago, when I was going through some kind of depression, I suppose.' He thought about it, I got the impression it may have been the first time he considered his habit.

'I remember the first time. It had been a few months ago that I had started avoiding people, living people, I suppose. I had been sleeping days and working nights, for weeks. That night I was at the bus stop. I let the first bus go. I could see it was too full, and I knew the next one came too soon after this one so it would be almost empty. I wouldn't have to share my seat. There is this glow that comes off a living body, and it was something I couldn't endure anymore. This day I was certain I could not bear it. I was right to have let the first bus go, the next one was almost empty.' I think at this point CC had forgotten it was me he was talking to. He seemed distant, almost as if he was telling me about someone else, not him, someone he knew well, but not himself.

'I had started out a bit early just so I could make sure I was comfortable on my way to work. It took long enough, and it made my day, or rather, night, better, if it started out well. There were two women sitting on the front seat, they were holding their bags in their laps. There their similarity ended. One had a skin type that deteriorated rapidly postmortem. The other was fat. It made everything yellow. You see? I think that's what it was. I had somehow begun to look at people as not-yet-dead.' He smiled at me, and then turned away, and continued talking absently again.

'I wasn't looking forward to my work that night. It was almost dinner time and I thought I wouldn't eat my packed dinner till after I was done. I can't work on a full stomach and hunger makes me work faster. I work in cold, you know that. That's great for a body from which life has just passed, but it's difficult on me, my fingers don't move as well. Anyway, I didn't know what was going to be on the table, because I'd been avoiding day shifts. So dad, or Uncle Carl, would leave a note for me, and I'd follow their instructions.'

I didn't know for sure, but, I'd seen him doing what he did, I didn't think hearing it in words would upset me much. I didn't think it would upset me at all, because, I kept thinking, the body he did what he did to didn't feel any pain.

'It was Sammy, from my college, before I quit—he was in my class, he had died in that bus crash, you know?' I did know. The driver had been drunk, he had taken the bus off the road in the ghats, it had landed almost a thousand feet down the valley, everyone had died.

'I'd loved Sammy for so long, from afar, and I knew he had died, but I hadn't seen him in two years. I had mourned him, when I heard, I'd cried a lot. It was such a shock, when I pulled out the freezer drawer, and it was him, I nearly fainted. I moved him to the work table, there was nothing much broken or anything. Just some bruises, I needed to do nothing much more than a bit of make-up, the funeral was in the morning. And I touched his face, without gloves, because I could, because I had wanted to for so long, because he wouldn't mind anymore, he wouldn't sneer at me, or call me a faggot.'

'He called you a faggot?' I asked, and he remembered it was me he was talking to. He nodded sadly, and said, 'Not many people did, people are kind mostly.

But Sammy, I think he knew how I felt about him, and maybe it just scared him. Maybe, he felt something. If not for me, but because maybe he was flattered. And that made him scared, and angry. So he lashed out. At me. Anyway. He was beautiful, laying there, cold, gone. And what can I say? I did the thing I wanted to do for years. And you'd think I'd mind that there was no response from my—lover—because that's what he was that night, but I didn't mind. I was relieved that he didn't push me away.'

I did understand. It was another side of what I felt—that Sammy did not want CC's love, or sex, when he was alive, and CC respected that. And CC waited till Sammy couldn't feel, before he took this chance, before he—had his way with him. CC fell silent. It was time to go, and we were done. I did have one thing left to say to him, a thought to put in his head. A favour to ask, in a way.

'I saw you look at my father that day, CC. When Penny. It'll be okay with me, you know,' I said, I didn't finish the sentence, and I didn't wait for a response. I was certain I had said enough, and that he understood. I walked away to the gate, I left him sitting on the bench, and I didn't look back, because I didn't want him to see the fiendish grin I felt splitting my face.

The funeral was three days later. The coffin was the best they had, there were flowers everywhere, it was all opulent and tasteful. CC had outdone himself, because I had inherited so much that the most expensive funeral service was not even a drop in the ocean. And because we were friends. And then I saw my father's face in the open coffin. He did not look peaceful. He looked subtly agonized, as if—as if he had not wanted what had been done to him, but he was powerless to stop it. I knew CC had understood what I had said, even before he came into the room and grinned at me. If he had ever been depressed, he wasn't any longer. And now, neither was I. I had honoured my father, the only way I could.

v

Beyond the Pale

You shall not kill.

Shweta drew her dupatta over her face to cover her nose. She fixated on the tracks silvery below her, feeling her eyes caught in a stare, but really her irises shimmered back and forth at high speed to the periphery of her vision and back. It was very early in the morning so it wasn't too crowded. Her journey across town was the opposite way from most people. She lived downtown and worked in one of those 'li'-ending suburbs, so far out that it was barely considered part of the city, so her ride was never too crowded anyway. The winter cold smothered the city with an intricate hanging particulate composed of a million slow and fast acting poisons. Warming fires in the track-side slums were kept alive by garbage and newsprint and anything that would burn.

She could smell things she knew she shouldn't allow
into her nose or lungs, things that evoked the military,
industry, pharmaceuticals, petroleum, heavy metals,
things with weight and no intent which would surely
kill her and everyone alive today. There were defecating
men and boys squatting along the tracks. They didn't
offend her as they used to. She didn't notice the faeces
piled up below them, nor their contribution to the air.
She hung in a trance as the train shuddered and lurched
its way to her destination. Her day would be quiet, she
worked in the library of a technical college, while she
earned her own degree there. After she graduated she
would look for a job closer to home, but there were
a couple of years to go still. She thought about her
husband. She always thought about her husband. If she
had passed him in the street, she would have turned her
head to look at him, and kept on looking till he was out
of sight. His boxy bleached white homespun shirts and
white hard-starched pants, the fine leather chappals, and
even if it wasn't his meticulous dress, his meticulous face
would draw her eyes, as it did every passing stranger's.
He was a blue stone Buddha statue come to life and
wandering the soiled streets of the city, floating just
off the grimy surface, untouched by the thickness
of the dissatisfaction and misery around him. Men
forgot, for a moment, when they looked at him. They
forgot their bedbug-infested mattresses, shit-smeared

toilets, the fingernail of soap that wouldn't conjure up a cleaning lather, the daily wage that wouldn't fit a new bar into its meagre bounds, they didn't remember the whiff of sourness from their wife's underarm as they turned quickly away and pressed their hands on her unwelcoming breasts and squirted a small guilty ejaculate into the thick condom, and then quickly, before they could see her disgust in the neighbour's light coming in through the barred window, turned away. Women forgot, the boredom, the pointless coupling, the slight prickly movement of the IUD, endless chopping of endless onions, the onion aura mingling with the hair oil that had become their signature scent, they forgot themselves, and the small hardness of their existence. His face somehow conjured up the delight in voices of small children eating guavas, and sweet gingered sugarcane juice quenching and cooling the throat, and a lungful of beedi on a cold night, and the actual spasm of release, that brief moment of pleasure when all the work of the day was done, that moment of being nothing. He did that to people. He did that to her too. Made her forget herself. She watched him, when he wasn't looking at her. She imagined them not married, strangers on a bus, or in the street. She imagined him bestowing his look on her. Just his look, nothing else. A passing glance of universal caring, blessing, not meant for her, just his look, as it passed over the world, passed over her. She

watched him when he wasn't aware of her, she looked
at his hands from under her eyelids, the long, elegant
brown fingers, the long nail beds, wrinkles precisely on
the knuckles and nowhere else, she looked at his blank
palms, three dark lines and nothing more, no confusion
of thought or cross hatches of desperation on those
hands, just like his face, untouched by wanton emotion
or desire. This was the man she saw when they were to
be married, this calm, benign, viceless face, and she, like
the rest of the world, mistook the workmanship of the
mask for benevolence in the man. He made her forget
herself. He made her forget, when she looked at his dark
heavily lashed eyes, that only hint to the aggression in
him, that she was small, thin, weak-breasted, barren,
ugly in every way a woman could be ugly. He made
her forget that her hair was lank and formless and
colourless, that her eyes, pink-tinged and lost in black
plastic frames and thick prescription dark glasses
could not stand the daylight, that her skin, shades of
white, covered in a shiny blonde down, sickened her,
because it sickened him. She forgot herself when she
looked at him. Her school days fell away, those days
of taunts and derision, insults about her white-cunt,
English-pig, but which were still validating, they were
still acknowledging of her. Better those words than the
fear-filled avoidance that sometimes took their place.
When she looked at her husband, she forgot her frantic

and forever search for colour in herself, her eternal prayer to the mirror to reflect back something other than paleness. She imagined herself as him, when she looked at him, imagined herself as dark, dark with the blue darkness of a god, her lips deep jamun-stained, her eyes, as his, shuttered with shades of thunder and coal, so rich with pigment, so saturated that it seemed it would rub off, she wished it would rub off onto her, she would forget her own translucence, opalescence, dead milk-cream-yogurt albino whiteness. Until he looked back at her.

And then the rattling train invaded her senses, and she hurtled down that tunnel of his disdain and loathing, she was scraped and gouged and yet contained forever in the cage of his contempt, mutilated even more than she already was from birth, by his hatred. There was a time when he was curious about her body, about the total lack of colour on her. He was curious, and fascinated. There was a time when she mistook his curiosity for attraction, and it was a kind of attraction, but not the kind she thought it was, and the fascination for devotion, because he was exquisitely fascinated by her. She thought wrong, but she responded to it, his searching, exploring, his examination of every inch, every pore of her achromatic flesh. He wanted to find colour in her too, she supposed, just like she herself did. He wanted her, when it first began. He had left marriage too late, and was too old for most, but she was almost as grateful as her parents when his mother broached the subject. They were married within weeks. He had consummated the marriage on that first night, in the dark, but the real journey began later, when his mother returned south to her hometown, and left them alone in his flat, in his bed. That very first night they were alone, he came back from the station, ate his dinner, and took her by her wrist to the bed and told her to lie down. He turned on all the lights in the room. Then he took off all her clothes himself, and though she was afraid, she said nothing, she lay motionless except for her breathing, drenched in anticipation and clenched in a sticky fever. He looked at her everywhere, lifting her arms, turning her this way and that. He looked at her eyes, her mouth, inside her mouth, as she had done too, all her life, the mirror showing her what she was. He looked at her small breasts, nipples, navel, ears, back, searching. She knew he would never find it, she was devoid of colour. And then he opened her legs and looked there, and she knew what he would see, she had looked at herself with small mirrors and large, ones with magnification and in all manner of rooms, and lighting conditions. He would see the white clitoris, almost transparent, the veins clear through the skin, the only colour in her was her blood. He would see the slickspace below, the same colourless shade as the substance that oozed from her because he was looking. He would see the hairs like threads of transparent plastic that curled all over her front and down the crack and around her white anus like the inside of a computer terminal. She thought of the day she had opened up a broken toaster to try and fix it, and she had cried out in horror when she found a cockroach inside it, as colourless and detailed as herself. She understood then what she had invoked all her life, for just a second. She had felt it. Revulsion. It was much greater than if it had been a normal dark insect with its thorned legs. It was an appalling whiteness. An all-encompassing flaw. Emptiness. She had smashed it to a pulp, and cried her heart out. And so he examined her, every night. And then every night, just like the first, he would abruptly release his indigo penis from its constraining fabric, hold it in his hand, and quickly turn off the light before engorging her with it, hurtling in and out of her until he had one of his violent, screaming orgasms that frightened her in their intensity, he screamed hoarsely every time and clutched at the sheets around her head. She tried to hold him that first night, and she moved a little, to participate, and he had stopped her with a harsh growl, forbidding her from touching him, ever. And it happened every night, until one day, even though she tried to stop him, he parted her milk thighs and found the colour of her womanness, just as she had found it that first time when she was fifteen. It had delighted her, that smear of perfect red seeping out of her, she stayed in the bathroom a long time with her legs apart and a mirror propped up in front of her, watching herself produce a colour, not just any colour, the colour of life. He was not delighted by it. He turned her roughly on her back and pulled her up in a face-down foetal crouch. Then he tried to grind the dark thing into her anus, first pushing and then thrusting, but he could not. She tried not to make a sound, but the pain escaped from her in a high wail of entreaty. He left her for a moment and returned with something cold that he applied to her behind, shoving it in with his fingers. Perhaps it was the scream that drew out his submerged malevolence—if she had stayed silent, she thought, this would have been a momentary incident, a failed attempt, done before she knew it. After her menses was done, he returned to his usual practice. And so it was, for a year. And one day, it changed. He stopped looking at her or touching her the way he used to. His touch now was only violent, he used his hands, his beautiful hands, dark against her blanched flesh. He would drag her against a wall, or throw her on the bed, he would rip off her clothes, he would hit her and kick her, but never hard enough to break skin, and then at some point he would become aroused, and masturbate. At first he went into the bathroom, but by and by he just stood over her as she lay on the floor or the bed, making no eye contact, ignoring her presence as the other children sometimes did when she was a little girl, and he would relieve himself, screaming in an agony of anger and horror. His revulsion had eclipsed his fascination. Still, she thought, it was her he sought out for this. And, by the end of the week, she was painted in all the hues of bruise from ink to marigold, from iris to sky, his fingers and palms and the soles of his feet left rainbows upon her breasts and hips and ribs and shoulders and arms and thighs. She admired them, and tracked their progress from birth to death, a coloured garden of flowers blooming and living and dying on the incandescent garden of her skin. He wanted her. She was the object of his desire. His desire, like everything else about him, was different from any other man's desire. And when she understood that, she was satisfied. She was in pain, but happy.

As the train left the city for cleaner tracks and the green smell of trees, Shweta readjusted her dupatta and wrapped it neatly around her ash blonde hair, and swung the ends over her shoulders. She had dressed in a blue flowered kurta which enhanced the blue tinge in her eyes and skin. She had put on mascara that morning, not black, but an ocean blue. She had read somewhere that blues were good for people like her. And today was the day visiting professors were coming from a university in the American North. She had looked forward to this all week, she knew she would enjoy the activities and festivities and special events. She would meet the four professors, and she would enjoy the fact that they would not react to her any differently than they did to anyone else. She had experienced this before, when the Norwegians came, and when the South Africans came. She found her fears of meeting new people were simply unwarranted when the new people were from outside. She had never left the country, but she wondered if there were so many freaks in their countries that people had stopped noticing, or if they had internalized difference as diversity to such an extent that even she would not only be accepted, but unnoticed. The idea thrilled her. She imagined walking into shops she had never been in before—something she never did, and talking to people normally the first time she met them—every time she met someone new. It was an irony that didn't escape her, that a colleague from the Delhi office was considered fair and therefore, beautiful, but she was a freak. Too fair. And it was this fairest of fair skin of hers, after all, that got her this husband, so beautiful, and his fascination for her. He would come back to her, and touch her as he used to. Her thoughts slowed with the slowing beat of the slowing train. But did she want him to? Touch her any other way than the way he did? Are two people closer than when one can cause the other pain, know a person well enough to cause pain? And derive such deep pleasure from that pain as to arrive at the pinnacle of pleasure through it? He would never find anyone like her, ever. Not in the world he inhabited, of a quiet back office, a world of rows and columns of numbers. He would never find someone he could despise as he did her. It was special and unique, their love. She would do whatever it took to be his victim. For him to be her master. For him to be a god, he needed her by his side, and in his bed. For him to be a god, she had to be his goddess, white shadow to his shadow darkness. The two of them were like the gods her grandmother prayed to. They were gods, and not like other mortals.

Professor Wyeth, Joan, was a woman with hair the colour of the polished copper pots and lingams in Shweta's grandmother's prayer room. It was cut shoulder-length. There were spots and dots and smudges all over her skin, on her face and nose, and the tops of her breasts which were two lovely little pillows disappearing into an emerald green T-shirt. She could not keep her eyes off this woman, and the woman seemed just as taken by her. Shweta was delighted when she was elected to show Joan around the library, and they were still on the tour at lunchtime. Joan said she didn't have to go back to the others, so Shweta invited her to sample the lunch buffet in the college cafeteria. They stood in line with large metal trays. Joan watched Shweta, and served herself exactly and only what she did. And then, as they sat at a corner table eating hot parathas and what she referred to as green goo, yellow goo and orange goo—aloo palak, daal, and chicken do piaza, thoroughly loving every bite, they became friends. Joan told her about her life back home in Syracuse, the snow, the lake effect, her hiking addiction, her little girl, her father who was a writer of self-help books. Shweta told Joan about her husband. There wasn't, and had never been anything else in her life worth talking about. Him, and her search for colour. And Joan wouldn't understand the latter at all.

They finished lunch, and when they went back to the conference room, someone had bolted the door from the inside. It was a mistake, of course, but they could hear the first post-lunch speaker being introduced, and didn't want to hammer on the door. Joan asked to use the restroom. Shweta knew by now that it was a toilet she needed. While Joan was inside the stall, Shweta washed her hands again to remove the smell of the chicken that clung to her fingers, and then pushed her sleeve up to check on the colours of her arm. Joan walked out just then. She took a sharp audible breath. Shweta covered up the arm, but it was done. Joan had seen her skin, mottled with old and new blue fingerprints, where his colour had rubbed off onto her. She wondered if she should retract her offer to show Joan the city, and to take her shopping that weekend, and her promise to introduce Joan to him, her beautiful husband. She couldn't find the words or the opportunity.

The day went by in a blur of excitement and delight, and Shweta realized she need not have worried at all about her friend's reaction. Joan was gentle and quiet and willing to have a good time, finding joy even when things went wrong. When the dish she ordered at lunch was too spicy and her face turned bright red, she laughed, wiping tears and eating pieces of what the waiter called boiled ice—meaning it was made of boiled water so it wouldn't make her sick. When they couldn't find the perfect shade of green to complement her red hair, Joan bought a black silk scarf saying it would make her fatty sister look good. She was lovely, and Shweta loved being with her. They were freaks, the pair of them, and it was easier to be one of a pair. And then, too soon, it was evening, and they took a taxi to the restaurant where they were to meet him. Shweta was quiet the whole way, and as the taxi slowed to a stop, Joan reached for her hand and squeezed it. Shweta didn't understand the gesture. She detected sympathy, and was puzzled, even angered by it. Joan would soon see him, her husband, and she would feel what everyone felt when they saw him. Belief in higher beings that walk among us. And Joan would see that Shweta needed no sympathy from anyone. That she was to be envied, not pitied, for she, the white freak, the transparent bug, she, and no other woman, shared this man's life. And she shared his bed. She brought him to the end of all his feelings, to the bottom of all his dreams, to the completion of all his wants. She owned his orgasms. She was the one complicit in his carnality. There would be no need for anything but envy to be felt for her, about her. And then there he was, and Shweta tore her eyes away from him to look at her friend as they stood at the entrance of the restaurant. Yes, Joan's eyes were upon him. And her eyes were glazed in the way everyone's eyes glazed when they encountered him. Joan clutched Shweta's arm suddenly, and tilted her chin, to show him to her. Shweta looked at him again, through this foreign stranger's eyes. Through this red-headed woman's forest green eyes. He sat there, by the window, looking out at the world, tall, dark, and so beautiful, the late evening sunlight almost unable to light up his darkness. She wanted to run to him there and then and kneel before him and make him look at her, she wanted to arouse his disgust and hatred from the root of his precious being, she wanted that dark part of him to rise there and then and demand her, her and no one else, and against his wish, he would have to have her. She remembered Joan, who was still waiting there in suspended motion, with her mouth slightly open. She had forgotten herself, as everyone else did. She was probably thinking about giving herself to him. She was imagining herself at his feet, naked and open, Shweta thought. She took Joan's hand and led her to the table. And introduced them. Joan was at a loss, she had not realized that the man she was looking at was Shweta's husband. Her face was hard to read, but the evening went well. He was, as always, charming, and attentive, but never in a focused way. Joan felt his benevolence upon her, a warm light on a dark day. She smiled and smiled, and if anyone had asked her what was said that day, she could not have told of anything but the calm in the eyes and the smile on the lips of a man she would never forget.

It was two years before Shweta saw Joan again. She ran into her unexpectedly on the steps of the university auditorium. It was an awkward moment, made worse by the bitter Syracuse cold. Shweta knew first-hand now what the lake effect was. She had seen it those past two winters. She would never forget her first snow. It was a short walk across dead lawns which, she had been told, would return in the spring, from the restaurant to her little second floor apartment. She enjoyed walking under the tall street lights, there were three dark steps from one circle of light to the next. Upstairs, she closed the curtains against the light right outside her window, and went to sleep. When she drew the curtains the next morning, she thought her whiteness had infected the world. Every last colour had vanished. The cracked black street, the distant red university buildings, the usually cobalt sky, the yellow windowsill, everything, near and far, everywhere her eyes could reach, was white. Snow had taken the world. She had smiled. She had felt at home, one with the white landscape.

Joan Wyeth had made it possible for her to be there. She had helped her apply, she had told her how to get finance, how a graduate student got work, she had done it all for her. And Shweta was grateful. Even though Joan had never understood her, she had meant well. Maybe it was she who didn't understand Joan, she sometimes thought. But it didn't matter now. Her husband was gone. He was dead, and it didn't matter anymore. She thought of those days sometimes, but not often, after he died, and the police came, and though she was never arrested or charged or taken to court, she felt a shudder of fear when she thought about it. She did not often think of the actual day. That was too much for her.

'I want a divorce,' he had said into the darkening spiral of her mind. She did not go back to those moments at all, if she could help it. 'Are you listening?' he asked again, and she was listening, but she did not understand. She began to take off her sari, she was wearing a sari that day. She took the pallu off her shoulder, letting it fall to the ground. If only he could see her naked, she thought, he would stop saying those

words. 'Stop doing that,' he said, taking a step towards
her. 'You have a job, a life. I need to get away from this.
It isn't right. I want a divorce. Please stop doing that,'
he said, as she unbuttoned her blouse and removed it,
a statue carved from a hunk of blue white marble, her
feet still unfinished, covered in the heap of sari. She was
still, waiting, naked, finally listening. He kept his eyes
on hers, looking into their colourless depths for the first
time in their life together. 'I can't go on like this, you
understand? I am hurting you, and you are unhappy,
and it is wrong,' he said. She wasn't unhappy, she said
to him, of course she wasn't, if that was what he wanted,
it was her privilege to give it to him, he could have her
any way he wanted, she was his wife, after all, she said
to him, tears of relief and love began to flow from her.
He thought she was unhappy, that's why he wanted to
leave her. For her own good. How wrong was he, she
thought, now everything would be fine. Forever. She
began to step towards him, so she could put her arms
around him, so she could give herself to him once again.
Maybe this time, now, finally, they could kiss, and he
could take her to their bed, and he could just lay on
her as a man, and she a woman, now that he knew.
And then his words: 'Stay away from me, don't do that
to yourself. Don't you understand? I don't want to feel
this way about you. I met someone else, a woman, a
normal woman, you know what I mean? I want to be

with her. I want a divorce. I want to be free from this—abomination.' And then she saw all the colours of the rainbow in her eyes and in her head, and she took the two steps forward and threw herself at him. He fell. He hit his head against the wall. He never stood up or walked or spoke again. He never touched her again.

When she met Joan at the airport that day she arrived, she was surprised at the reception. Joan enveloped her in a hug. Later, when they arrived and she was settled in her apartment, they had talked. Joan broached the subject as she was getting ready to leave. 'You poor girl, you poor girl, what you've been through... I can't imagine... but you know I understand. I would have done the same thing, if I had half the guts you did. That bastard, I saw what he did to you... it was self-defence, I know.' And Shweta asked her, 'What do you mean, Joan? What he did to me?'

'I saw your arms, and the bruises. I know how that is.'

'That's not it, Joan. He was my husband, I was his wife. That was how he showed his love. That's not what hurt me at all.'

'What then?' Joan asked, clearly puzzled. 'What made you—do what you did?' Shweta had tried to explain to her friend, but she hadn't understood. Joan had only stared at her in shock, and then stood up and walked out. They had never spoken again, till that cold morning on the auditorium steps. Shweta was the puzzled one at the end of it. She had told her friend the truth, she didn't know what else she could have told her.

'It was another woman. He had another woman. He wanted a divorce, Joan, he wanted to leave me. For another woman. That's why I did it.'

vi

Fall

You shall not commit adultery.

Srinivas sat on the black leather sofa next to his best friend's wife. He did not turn his head or move. He was not aware of his silence or stillness, because he could hear his blood pouring through his veins and slamming into his heart like the Niagara river on the rocks below. His thoughts had stopped entirely, deafened by his physical reaction to what Jenna had just said. He swallowed, because his tongue felt thick and his throat had begun to close. He closed his eyes. The sound of his heart threatened him inside the darkness of his head, and he quickly opened them again. He could still feel her sitting next to him, but he did not turn to look at her in the gloom of the fading day. He felt himself falling into a hole of memory, of pain and longing, skins began to peel off haphazardly as he plunged. Yesterday, at Niagara, her hair, cascading, tumbling out of the black wool cap onto her shoulders, her green eyes squinted against the cold, her skin, he wanted to reach out and touch it, he knew it would be cold under his hot fingers, but he just held his cup of mocha as she took his picture with his back to the falls, the wind cutting through them. A few huddled Koreans, trees with no leaves standing naked, the falls frozen in bits, like him, beginning to seize as the winter of his loneliness took hold. The drive there, the colours muted by snow, speaking to him in whispers, so he had to watch and listen, the hawks everywhere, palely marked, like giant moths against a bright grey sky, lakes, the Welland canal, cold outside, warm inside the car, Jenna at the wheel beside him, taking him somewhere to show him something in some corner of the world. He looked out of the window on her side, but saw only her. Her hair, her mouth, her hands. The persistence of his longing was like a burn on his retina. He could see, but only through it. He could live, he had lived, but only in its presence, this endless longing, with him since the first moment he saw her.

That was then, twenty-five years ago, he was twenty-two years old, his friend had come home, to show his new wife to his beloved country. Srinivas, running down the stairs of his parents' house when he heard his mother calling Ravi was here, and he saw her, Jenna, and his breath had stopped, and he had never quite caught it again since. Green eyes looking up at him, a huge smile on her happy face, her glorious hair, her delight, and the beginning and end of his. He laughed at himself that night laying in his bed after they had spent the day together, because what else could he do, after falling in love with his best friend's wife, what else was there to do but laugh. That was probably the last time he laughed about it. He thought, they would leave, go back home to their life in the cold north, he would go back to the mad heat of Mumbai, his job, he would dream of her again, for sure, but that would be that, and time, a week, would rub out his infatuation. There would be some of it left, of course, she was too lovely to be forgotten, and he would always know her, of course, because she was Ravi's wife, and Ravi would always be in his life, and they would even be good friends some day, Jenna and Srinivas, he thought. In the shower that night, he conjured up what he had seen of her body, a smudge of skin between bra strap and dress, a classic look inside the front of her dress at the swells of her breasts, it was her hair, he had never seen anything that colour, which flashed in his imagination even as the hot water washed away the remains of his infatuation. And that was the last time he had allowed himself to think of her in that way, he felt a kind of uncomfortable betrayal, and he didn't do it again.

But then the job brought him to Los Angeles, and then Atlanta, and Ravi and Jenna, and then Ravi and Jenna and Megan were one flight away in Toronto, and there it was again. Seeing her again, a not-so-old, not-so faded picture repainted in vibrant new colours so they glowed, more glimpses into her eyes, her life, her dress, drives through Ontario wine country, Ravi asleep in the back seat, just him and Jenna talking, laughing, she touched his hand sometimes as she said something, his skin blistered, her hair in the wind when they hiked through a gorge north of Atlanta, he caught her once when she slipped, late evening, after a noon of wine, many friends, old college friends from five years at Hostel 4, wives, some from back home, some from this new country, him, Srinivas, then still single, and the only single man there, she took a false step in her pale green high-heeled shoes, began to fall forward, he caught her, by the waist, and her face was close to his, his face was in her hair, and he took a deep breath, the first in years. She turned and smiled at him and thanked him, and he almost forgot to let go of her, Jenna, and he knew why he didn't think of her when he had the little two-week layovers with various women, or even when he jerked off in the shower, he knew why he avoided thoughts of her, because they were feelings of her, because she was his dearest friend's wife, because she was Jenna, because he loved her.

'Fuck me, Srinivas.'

Had she really said that? Or was it just a part of a fantasy which had sat in him unopened and untouched for two decades, and was breaking out now in spite of his best efforts? Ravi had gone on an unscheduled trip, and there he was, with Jenna and Megan, sixteen, who had grown into a smart, talkative teenager, always on her way out, always texting on her fancy phone, three whole days in a huge house which was beginning to close in. He had woken early, let the cat out, made himself coffee, chatted and eaten toast with Megan before her ride to school honked loudly outside, sent out emails, he had an exhibition coming up, and he had to liaise with transporters and packers for his rather huge pieces. It was funny how his art was beginning to make him more money than his job these past few years, his five years at engineering college were reaching the end of their usefulness finally. By the time Jenna came down from her and Ravi's bedroom it was almost ten, and she was very happy that he had made himself at home, and even happier to curl up on the couch with the cup of coffee he handed her. And the rest of their day had been spent mostly on the couch, she sat at one end and he at the other, both with their laptops, talking occasionally, eating a snack every so often, drinking coffee till it was all gone. At dinner time he said he would cook, and he did, he stir-fried shrimp he found in the freezer with a chopped-up habanero, and cilantro, and segments of cucumber and bits of pecan, and he served it to them both on brown rice. She was amazed and delighted. She finished the whole plate, she had two glasses of wine, he knew she loved her pinkish Zinfandels which he found unpalatable, but loved that she drank it, a silly pink wine. She put the glass down, she put her empty plate on the coffee table, she turned towards him, her arm on the back of the couch almost touching him. Then she leaned forward and kissed him on his mouth. And his blood began to pound in his head. And he was not sure what he did and didn't hear after that.

He thought about the six-year relationship he had ended just before this visit. It had not been a bad relationship at all, except for her incessant insecurity, her constant need to know where he was and with whom and why. Classic, really. And if he had loved her, he would have even put up with it, built a sense of security in her. Sara. But he hadn't. He just hadn't loved her enough. Or at all. His mother was disappointed when he had told her it was over. She had thought there would be marriage, and hoped there would be children. She thought he had left it too long, they should have married much sooner. But Sara had a job, a career she didn't want to interrupt with marriage and children, yet. Well, it was too late. And wherever his thoughts went in the past, they came back here, to the couch, to Jenna, to what he would do or would not do, he knew this was the beginning of a new hell. He knew it.

He turned to look at her finally. Jenna's hair, that he wanted so much to push his hands and face into, and her green eyes, he would look into them when he did what she asked him to, there was such pleading in those eyes that it shocked him. She smiled. 'Sex is easy, isn't it, Srini? We can go to your room, please, and stay in bed all day and all night and all tomorrow, and then we can go on with life, what's changed? Except we'll both be a bit happier?' What was he going to say, he wondered. Even if Ravi had not been his friend, even if he had not spent his childhood, his college years, his youth with him, still, still, this was his house, his hospitality, his trust, his woman, his wife, and Srinivas began to realize the extent of this landscape of his new home, his new acreage in hell. She leaned closer to him, her mouth, Jenna's mouth, making small, perfect kisses around his mouth, little breaths brushing his mouth, she trailed tiny kisses down his neck, his descent a trajectory of a Dylan song, darker, more beautiful, all the old desire, the final layers of him peeling off, his control vanishing, his morality, his friendship, his right and wrong in pieces, gone all to dust.

'Jenna,' he said. 'No.'

She drew back, in anger. He opened his mouth, and she put her hand on it. 'I heard you. You said no. There is nothing else to say. I've heard it before. I wasn't asking you to love me, Srinivas. Just to want me a little. To be a man. To lie with me.'

A smile, then, and her voice became soft, and cold, he had never heard it like that before, 'Lie with me. Funny. A Freudian slip. I meant to say lay with me. But if you lay with me, you'll have to lie with me too. He doesn't give a damn who I sleep with Srini, why should he? He hasn't said yes to me in years. And you are like brothers, all you men. No? No what? No, you won't kiss me? Why? Is my mouth all wrong for you? Won't it fit on yours? Won't fit on your cock, Srinivas? Why, don't you think I can please you? Am I too old? Forty-three too old? No what?'

Srinivas took a breath quickly. He loved her, and he couldn't fuck her. He answered her, honestly. 'No, I can't fuck you, Jenna. No, not because you are not the most beautiful woman I have ever known, not because I haven't thought about nothing but you these twenty years since the first day I saw your face, not even because Ravi is my friend and I won't disrespect him, Jenna. Though all this is true, I won't fuck you, because I love you. I know how it will be, my love. I know how we will be together, I know how you look at me, and how I look at you, I know we will touch and all our moments will be perfect, I know we will fit together, my love, I know we will breathe together, and sleep together and our fuck will be love and sweetness, my love, Jenna, my love. All this I know is true.

'But it isn't why I won't fuck you. I won't, because I won't go home tomorrow after this day and night with you, and sit in my room after this, day after day, night after night, week after week, year after year, wishing for you because I have known you, and wanting you, and dying from this love. I can't.'

And he put his fingers in her hair, and he pulled her close to him, and he kissed her, and she kissed him, deep and long, and deeper, and longer, and he began to pull away, and she wouldn't let him go, she put her arm around his neck, she slipped below him, she put her legs around his waist, she moaned his name, she said, 'Oh please, please ...' And he held her arms, and separated them from each other. She sat up, and arranged herself, pushing her hair away from her face. 'It's fine, I get it,' she said. And he heard bitterness. And his sorrow showed in the shine in his eyes, but she was angry. 'You said no. And you won't do it. You think of yourself. And your future misery. And your friend. And your honour. And mine. And betrayal? You think you will betray your friend? And what? I'm his property, that you cannot use? Like driving his car? What if you drove his car? Or fucked his wife? And anyway, I'm not his car. I'm me. If I want to fuck you, that's what I want. It has nothing to do with him. Or you.' She was clenching her fists, and her jaw was hard together and she spoke through her teeth, almost hissing, full of poisonous anger that he knew had nothing to do with him, or his no. But he had to listen to her, and see this through, whatever it was.

'No. You say, no. Why? Why can't we just do it? And forget it till some other time? Do you want me to beg? I will, if you want. I know you want me, Srinivas, and you know right now I want you. You know I've thought about it a lot, I know you have too, and now we can do this. We are adults, Srini, I need someone who loves me, who is my friend, to do me this favour. Will you not do it?'

He was lost. He had stumbled onto something he was not prepared for. He knew what it was, but he could not name it. She was in a state of passion so beautiful that he would have had her there, in that moment, on that couch, and why not, her mouth was so soft, her breasts, she had no bra on, her nipples, he could see them, her legs, strong around his body a few moments ago, he hard and ready and willing, why not, he thought. But he knew this thing she was feeling. Her whole body quivered with a desire, and a need, this woman, angry for having to ask, he knew what this was. Her desire, deep and desperate, it was not for him. She wanted to be held, and touched, and wanted, and she wanted to be told she was wanted, by look and words and touch and frantic orgasms, over and over. And he knew it would be that way, with them. But her desire, it held him back even more than fear for his life without her. Her desire was for herself, for her, she wanted to know herself, find herself, unlock herself.

He was puzzled as he watched her, standing there, her anger fading, she was not even aware of her tears wetting her cheeks. How could this be, he thought. Twenty years, since she was a young girl, he had known her. She was without a doubt beautiful. By any standard, by any stretch. She was beautiful, and motherhood and age had made her more beautiful. There were lines around her mouth and eyes that he adored, she wasn't the slim young girl she'd been, but the sixteen years since she had Megan had put curves on her, and he stopped himself there. His long years of hunger licked up into him, and he was glad when she said she had to take some clothes to Megan in school because she was spending the weekend at a friend's. He said he would tidy up and take a shower.

'I'll be about an hour,' she said, 'I may have to drive all the girls, and I'll pick up a couple of steaks and wine for dinner. You can grill, can't you?'

'In the snow?' Srinivas asked her, a bit confused.

'No, on the indoor grill, I'll show you,' she said, and she picked up her bag and keys and left, and he didn't sense much anger trailing her. He picked up the coffee cups and newspapers and tidied up a bit. He went to his room and took out fresh undies and a T-shirt. He looked around for a towel but didn't see one. He wondered if he should wait for her or go upstairs and find one. He had been upstairs before, he had sat with Ravi and drunk beer in the den and watched football while she slept in their bedroom across the hall. There was no reason why he shouldn't go up and find a towel. He went. There was no towel in the den or hallway, and, as he had known he would have to, he went into the bedroom. It was as he remembered it, a dark green Rajasthani quilt covered the bed, a desk stood at the window, an open notebook drew him there immediately. He bent to look. He realized that he knew her handwriting because she had written to him, every Christmas, every Diwali, she was the one who wrote in a pretty card and signed for herself and Ravi. He stood there, wondering how much he really knew about her.

'I'll read it to you,' he heard her voice from the door. He turned, and was embarrassed, and angry with himself, and tried to tell her he had not read, nor intended to read. But he said nothing, there was no point.

'Sit,' she said, 'I'll read what I wrote last night.' He didn't sit. He wanted to leave the room. He just stood there, looking at her hair, and the return of her anger. She said again, 'Sit, Srinivas. I want you to understand why I said what I said, why I want what I want, and why I am so angry.'

'Can't we go downstairs?' he asked her, smiling a little. She smiled too, and said, 'Oh all right, go. I'll come down in a minute, I have to pee. Srinivas, what were you doing in my bedroom anyway?'

'I wanted a towel, would you bring me one please?'

He went downstairs and got a glass of water. He considered for a moment that he could have said yes, and would have spent the afternoon, and now the evening, and all night in the arms of the woman he had wanted for two decades. He wished he could crush his conscience, and crush her, in his grip, in his arms. He took a few shaky breaths, and sipped his water. She came to the kitchen, and sat at one of the barstools across from him. She had her book, she opened it up in front of her.

'Marinate the steaks, that way you will have your back to me while I speak to you,' she said. But he sat down in front of her with a bottle of wine and a glass, just one. She looked at the page. And then she really began to read from it.

'I fantasize about rejection the way other people fantasize about pain. What else can I do now, when that's all I have ever had?' She stopped. She looked at him. 'Just come to my bed, or let me come to yours. It's been so very long, since someone said yes to me, Srini. Be the one.'

He got up and went around to where she sat, her

tears had begun again. He put his arms around her and she leaned back against him. He put his face in her hair, Jenna's hair, and he knew, there was no going back. He had tried, in some small way, and he had failed. He gave up, and gave in, and she felt it. She stood up, and put her arms around him. The moment he looked at her, like that, all his love was there, between them, all of it, from the years and years before, thawed, and boiling over. He took her hand and took her to his bed. There was a moment of uncertainty. For them both. Her need to feel drowned it all. She led him, into her darkness.

∼

Jenna walked into the guest room of her house with her husband's best friend. She closed her eyes a moment. Srinivas. She had said words to him she had never said to any man, ever. She did not know how else to ask. Four years had gone by, since she stopped. Stopped what? When they had married, Ravi and she, she had been so very very happy. She saw photos of herself at the wedding, the party in Hyderabad, the party in Toronto, where all her sisters and brothers and mother and father and uncles and aunts and cousins came. Young and full of anticipation of the sweetness to come. That night, they stayed at her parents' place, and everyone slept all over the house, but they had the guest bedroom, and she was thrilled.

Of course they had slept together, for two whole years, but this was their wedding night. She undressed and slipped into the bed and curled up against him, already feeling wet and warm in anticipation. He kissed her, and she thought it would be the loveliest sex they had ever had. And then he turned her a little, so she was facing away from him, and put his leg over her, and said, 'Sleep well.' She was too stunned to say anything, but she was tired, and soon fell asleep. And then there was sex, of course, and some of it was sweet, and there was Megan, and there was school, and her own PhD, and his father's sickness, and then she was just not the main thing, not even to herself. And then, every time they met Srinivas, and every time she turned to look at him and found his eyes on her, with such a look in them as she never saw on Ravi's face, a clear and transparent ache for her, she would open up, she would remember that she was a beautiful and sexy woman. She would believe what the mirror sometimes showed her, a toss of wild loose red curls, slanty green eyes, a face that was older than young, but not as old as old, waiting for a man's urgent touch, sweet touch, loving touch, aggressive touch, demanding touch, because he wanted her. Srinivas wanted her. Ravi had said no in so many ways. He was tired, he was late, his parents were in the next room, his head hurt, he was busy, he had to wake up early the next day, he didn't feel like it. And one day, she stopped asking. If she had said to him, 'Ravi, please just fuck me,' she wondered, if he would have, if he would have understood the urgency she felt, and the danger that she was almost lost to him. But she never did ask that way. So now here she was, in their guest bedroom, in their own house, she had said to this man, who had wanted her so long, whom she knew she would hurt, whom she would use and destroy, 'Srinivas, fuck me. Sex is easy, we can do this.'

She took her dress off over her head, she unhooked her bra, she dropped it to the ground, her breasts dropped slightly, but he stepped towards her and put both his hands on them, and he bent down and kissed her. Then he just looked at her face, and there was an amazement, a wonder in his face as he did, childlike and quiet, he brought her to lie on the bed. He pulled a blanket over them, and kissed and kissed her and said, over and over, 'You are so beautiful, Jenna, and I have wanted you so much, my love, my life,' he kissed her, all of her, he forgot no part, he neglected no little inch of her skin and her being. Not her face, her crazy green eyes, not her breasts, not her back, which he lay on, not her hair, which he had lost himself in, and not the sweet little strip of red curls he found under her green panties. Those he kissed, and reached inside with his tongue, and she held his hands, and raised her hips to him, and suddenly pulled him all the way up.

'Look at me,' she said. 'It's been so long, and it's so sweet, and I don't want to feel this alone,' she said, pushing his hands down, and his fingers, with hers, inside her, where his tongue had just been. She looked deep into his eyes, and as they sunk their fingers deeper and deeper inside her, together, he saw it in her eyes, her orgasm, long before he felt those little and then huge contractions as she finally moaned, and said 'Kiss me, my love.'

~

He took an early flight home. He had a message from her on his cell phone when he touched down in Atlanta. And later an email, with an attachment. He opened it up. He stood holding a cup of Tim Horton's hot cocoa. He smiled sadly into the camera. It was the sad smile of a clear conscience. The Niagara river plunged down behind him, as it had done forever before, and would do forever after him.

vii

Wakulla

You shall not steal.

Eddie moved to the right of the highway, the slow lane. It was a long drive, but a lovely one, and he didn't want the stress of speed to interfere with his enjoyment. The high green walls of the Apalachicola National Forest rose on both sides of the broad road. He could discern no variation in shade, and unbroken cloud cover deepened the greenness of the kudzu-covered trees. His church was a two-hour drive. Though he could cut fifteen minutes by driving in the fast lane, he just didn't do it that way. His Ford pick-up was ancient, and he even had vintage Florida plates, so people didn't try to make him go any faster by tailgating or honking at him, they just went around him, and he puttered on, taking his time. Wakulla County's only Catholic, and not a very devout one, it had been two months since his last time in church. But this Sunday was his birthday, a big one, so he thought he would go, this would be the day, when he did the things he had left undone. Half a century old, he thought. In his fifty years he hadn't moved even fifty miles away from where he was born and went to school, he was still inside the Wakulla County line.

He would have missed the little car if it hadn't been offensively red—it was like a fresh drop of blood against the green. It looked as if it had slid off the pavement into the grassy embankment, he could see the smooth brown scars on the green where the tyres had skinned off the grass. There seemed to be no one about. He turned on his hazards and slowed, and then stopped, as far off the road as he could without sliding off the gentle green slope himself. He took his cell phone out of the glove and got out of the pick-up to take a look, and a young man came out of the passenger side of the car.

'Are you doing okay?' Eddie called out over the sound of wind and traffic, and the man waved as he came towards him.

'Thank you for stopping, I'm okay,' he said. Eddie looked him over. He seemed barely sixteen, and he hadn't been in the driver's seat, but there was no one else near, so Eddie asked, 'Can I see your licence and registration please, sir,' holding up his own badge. The young man, to Eddie's relief, looked quite relieved himself. That was always a good sign, when a person was relieved rather than anxious to see a policeman.

'Oh, I don't have one, my dad's gone to look for help, he was driving. I have a permit,' he said, and went to the car to get it. Eddie stood waiting, his hands on his hips, and by the time the boy came back there was a police car behind them, lights flashing. Eddie shrugged and started back to his truck. His colleagues from the highway patrol would take care of it.

'Eddie? Eddie Longbow?' Eddie turned around and the officer's face crinkled up in happiness. 'Eddie!' he said, and ran up and put his arm around Eddie's shoulders and then pushed him aside to look at him, he was so ebulliently happy that Eddie was embarrassed, and then worried, that he couldn't remember ever having seen him before.

'You saved my life, Eddie,' the big man said, 'I don't think you know who I am,' and he laughed and kept hugging Eddie and shaking his head. His partner came out of the car, she was curious, and the man explained to her that Eddie had saved his life. Eddie was confused, still not remembering.

'I was fourteen, you pulled me out of the river—oh hell, there's no way you would know who I am, I was smaller than my leg. We lived out by Wakulla then, but I always wanted to meet you and say thank you, I've had your picture in my room since back then. You are Eddie Longbow, yeah?' he asked, a bit late, Eddie thought.

'Yeah,' he said, laughing, relieved to know what it was all about. He stepped back from the man and held out his hand for a shake, and a proper introduction.

'George Saeed,' the man said, 'Why did you pull over? Do you have a problem? I should have asked that first, look at me, sorry.'

'I only stopped to see if the young man here was all right,' Eddie said, and began to back away, he wanted to be back on the road, or he would miss mass. George wasn't ready to let him go though.

'Call me?' he said, holding out his card, and Eddie took it, and smiled, but said nothing.

Eddie never doubted the truck, it had never failed him. The key turned and there was the gruff clearing of the throat and then the soft endless metal vibration under his feet, all through his arms and in his teeth, sound and feeling joined to themselves and to his body mile after mile of highway, byway, dirt and tar, forever. He loved his truck, and it seemed to him the truck loved him. Not that Eddie would actually ever give an automobile life or feelings, it was more of a sense that the truck was his, and would not let him down.

Pulling people out of water was something he had had to do a lot of, in Wakulla, where land was never far from it, the dark water, lousy with alligator. He had swum in it regardless, all his life. It wasn't something he thought about, never had, and nor had anyone he knew.

Everyone just did what they wanted, or had to, and he
didn't know anyone personally or by hearsay who had
suffered a bite, let alone death by 'gator. People, now,
that was a different thing. People certainly killed more
people than any 'gator. The house where he was born,
where he grew up, sat an energetic stone's throw away
from the swamp on one side and the river, the Wakulla
river, bounded the property on one side, so 'gator on the
property was a common occurrence. But neither he nor
his siblings, nor anyone in the family in all the almost
eighty years they had owned the place, had ever been
hurt by one. His great-grandfather had killed a Seminole
gentleman for falling in love with his daughter, too
late, she was already carrying the man's child. And his
uncle on his father's side had strangled his wife, when
she tried to get away from her drunk, crazed husband.
No, it wasn't 'gators that presented the most danger in
Wakulla, it was people. Men mostly.

George Saeed. Eddie remembered something of the
incident, but not much. It was probably at the spring,
where ten thousand gallons of water are added to the
river every second, and he and his mates had snuck into
the park on summer afternoons to fling themselves from
the high platform that jutted out right over the spring,
where it was deepest below them. It was the greatest joy
of his entire life, the scream that rose from his belly, cut
off as he landed in the cool dark green water. 'Gators

sunned themselves on the far side, oblivious to the small flying bodies, they never came to the area where the spring was. Probably too cold for reptilian blood. When had he stopped jumping into the Wakulla, Eddie wondered. When he was through school, probably, and there were no more summer breaks. And life happened and this job, and then no more breaks at all.

Eddie didn't remember having learned to swim. Living near the water, on the water, even water that was 'gator infested, meant knowing how to breathe in it, float in it, travel in it, from a very young age. He went fishing with his father and uncles on school holidays. His father didn't have to call him twice, he would leap out of bed and creep out of the house at four in the morning when all the world except fishermen slept under slowly swirling fans in sweaty sheets. They would spray themselves head to toe in mosquito repellent, and he would ride in the bed of the truck, sometimes with the dog, out to the water's edge, and then they would drag the boat into the water and make their slow chug downriver to the lighthouse. There the Wakulla lost itself in the Gulf of Mexico, and there, at the edge of the ocean, a lifetime ago, he met Craig, and his young Indian wife Ray. Revati. Indian, not Seminole Indian, really from India, a country Eddie could not even begin to imagine. They stood there, hand in hand, and Eddie had felt a strange confusion within himself, because they seemed so right together, and yet, everything he had been told all his life, said that it was unnatural.

The memory brought him a smile, and then the tears. He took the exit off the highway and drove into the first fast food place he saw. The line was long but he needed a coffee. When his turn came he got a whiff of fried chicken and got himself a spicy sandwich with extra pickles, and coffee with three sugars, and then parked to eat. He knew he would miss mass, but that's not what he was going for anyway. A large flock of Canada geese strutted in the field behind the drive-through. They were Florida geese now, he guessed, they didn't bother going home anymore. The line of fast food places and gas stations were like a movie set, he thought, just a road, the single file of buildings on both sides, and behind them, fields, and then the forest, hopefully forever, the forest. Craig had loved walking in the dark trees. They would walk all day, sometimes, after a big breakfast, the two of them. Oftener than Eddie cared to remember, the day ended with them stuck under a live oak as the sky pounded them with rain and they could neither speak nor smoke because it was so thunderously loud and so wet. The lightning both terrified and delighted them, and he remembered the relief after the storm had passed, when they would squelch back to the truck and drive home, swearing they would never do it again. They always saw animals, white-tailed deer, an armadillo, turtles, and enough times, 'gator. Craig would clutch his arm, he always spotted them, they would back away. In all their rambles through the woods, they had never been chased by anything. Boar, bear, fox, and once, just the once, a red panther, but the animals were less threatened by them than they should be. They could have been hunters. There were enough of those.

Craig had been chased down in the end, in Mosul, where Eddie wasn't with him, and his body came back in a closed box. Eddie had held Ray in his arms as she lost control, and then consciousness. They hadn't been close, Eddie and Ray, she was always Craig's wife to him. He was fascinated by her at first, of course, as Craig must have been. Two boys from Wakulla County, and she the Oriental princess they had seen in animated films, with her strange matte skin and long blue-dark braid that moved like a captured snake on her spine as she walked, and her eyes, so very black. Eddie couldn't imagine being with such a person. She was far too foreign for him, far too—exotic, and she hated it when he said that word. She made him aware of things within him that he never knew he had, racism, sexism, she even proved to him that he was a misogynist. He was always uncomfortable around her, and by the time he understood that she was beautiful, he was used to her. He was convinced that they were made for each other, Ray and Craig, the dark princess and the awkward red-headed kid from the backwaters of north Florida. He would watch them, glancing at their entwined hands, or her head against Craig's, or when they all swam together, and he could see those bodies against each other, Eddie liked that the best. It wasn't sexual, not at all, he just got such pleasure from the sheer impossibility of the sight. The dissonance delighted him where it would jar or even offend other people. He would sit at the shore and just watch them, like he watched manatees, or turtles, just for the joy of it.

One fishing Sunday he arrived as usual, to pick up Craig. Craig always left the front door open, so Eddie wouldn't wake Ray when he came, it was usually 4 am, and Craig was never ready to go, though he was always up. Eddie looked, the bathroom window was dark. He figured Craig had forgotten the alarm, and went quietly up the stairs. He heard the sigh and knew what it was, but his hand was already pushing open the door. Against the early morning gloom at the window, there they were, a pale morph and a dark, red-tailed hawk fluttering alongside each other, she on top of him, his pale hands on her dark, sloping breasts, her braid alive, moving like a snake as she moved, the gloom brightening as they moved, so slowly, the languor of half-sleep made the scene seem like a slow motion dream in sepia. Eddie enjoyed watching them, even as they woke up a little, even as they stroked and kissed and sighed a little louder, even as Craig became urgent in his need to come to orgasm, perhaps aware Eddie would be there soon, he nudged her over, and she arched like a panther and let him, and even then, they were animals in the wild to Eddie. He felt nothing but that, the joy of watching deer high-jumping through the forest, hawks in the sky, wheeling and playing on the winds. He touched his penis through his pants, just to make sure, though of course he didn't need to. When he thought about it later, and again, and again, it was the same. He felt only the excitement and delight of finding a pair of raptors living in his yard, the female with abnormal plumage. He was grateful to have seen what he had seen, the wild beauty of it. But after Craig was gone, it illuminated his loss, and his understanding of hers. He could see down into the heart of it. Like, back when he was a boy, the Wakulla was as yet unsullied by human effluents, and he could look into its pulsing heart, the spring itself.

The Wakulla. Love, life, death, he had received everything from those waters. He had pulled George Saeed from the river alive. He suddenly remembered the day. Warnings had been issued, it was hurricane season, the waters were high, no one heeded them. Schools were on summer break, the whole state was in the water somewhere—it was over a hundred degrees, the water was the only place to be, unless you were on a couch in air-conditioning. There were calls coming in constantly. It wasn't at the spring, as he had thought. They had received the call in the middle of the day, and he had been close to the spot, it was a bridge, and kids were jumping off it into the river below, as they always did. This boy had hit his shoulder on the side as he flung himself, not far enough from the concrete, and was being carried downriver fast. When Eddie found him he was in trouble. A good swimmer, but with just one working arm, he was losing his struggle. Eddie took off his belt and handed it to his partner, and then jumped in and brought the boy out. It wasn't dramatic or loud, there was no one about but his partner on the shore, they put him in the car and brought him back to the rest of his party, there was cheering, Eddie left. George Saeed, Eddie hadn't remembered his name, he had only to write it once on the report, and he had forgotten it. It was the time when Craig had gone to Iraq, or come back, dead, and Eddie didn't really remember anything from that time.

No. That was untrue. He remembered what needed to be remembered. And what needed to be forgiven. He gathered up his food wrappers and placed them in the paper bag, and threw them into the trash as he passed it. He was back on the highway, the engine snoring sweetly. The landscape was different here, it was more open, agriculture on both sides of the broad road, more traffic, and he was forced to speed up just a little, he knew if he was under the limit a colleague would pull him over. He admitted to himself why he was going to church this particular Sunday. His birthday, but also, he knew it was safe now, to talk.

Eddie had been at their house the night before Craig left. The evening was no different from any other, Craig had grilled mullet from the freezer that they had caught together the week before, Ray had made aloo gobi that she knew Eddie enjoyed, and raita, and they drank a lot of beer, and they talked about this and that and everything and anything at all except Iraq, except the only thing that they were all thinking, that Craig would leave in the morning, and that Craig may never come back. Eddie could see it in her eyes, in her shaky hands, in her quiet, Ray was terrified. She was also two months pregnant. After dinner, it was Craig who usually cleaned up and put things away, but Ray said, 'You guys go sit outside and talk, I'll do the dishes,' so they had gone out. Eddie had meant to leave right after dinner, he hadn't wanted to take time from their last evening together. But Craig made him sit on the porch. Fireflies pulsed under the moss-laden oaks, and they said nothing in the loud silence of the forest. The sound of the cicadas rose and fell and rose and fell and finally Craig spoke, with his hand on Eddie's arm.

'You'll look in on her?'

'I will,' Eddie had said, because he knew Ray had no

one else. Craig's family was no different from his own. Eddie's family would erase the Seminole stain in their line if they could, they rarely even admitted it. Craig's mother, his father often said, was lucky she had died rather than live through the shame Craig had brought upon them. Ray laughed at all this, she said it was no different from where she came from. Tribes, she said, no matter where one came from on this rotten earth, will tear each other down. She rarely spoke of it, but when she did, it was with such deep bitterness that it made Eddie cringe, and made him feel ashamed for his country, and for humanity.

Eddie did not go look in on her, until Craig called him one time, and asked. Eddie promised Craig, and himself, that he would not say 'no I haven't' the next time Craig called. He made it his Sunday ritual, to pick up Ray, drive her to church, and then have lunch with her. It was awkward at first. They both realized how much it was Craig who connected them, how little they knew about each other, and how little they had in common. And then, into the awkward silence, she commented on how lovely his engine sounded. He didn't even think about it as he launched into the story of his truck, the old Seminole who sold it to him, how he took care of it, the tale of every dent and scratch it had ever received, the one small accident he had had when a fourteen-year-old learner had bumped into him at a stop light, and suddenly they were at her house. They both burst out laughing. It was the last time they were awkward together. He watched her child grow within her each week, and every week when Craig called for a report, he had one to give. It was a beautiful time, the growing friendship between them bound up by their mutual love for Craig, and yet, shot through with feelings of anxiety from both of them because he was out there in the world, at war, in mortal danger.

How is it, Eddie thought, that he didn't see it coming, that he didn't understand that trajectory, just as surely as if he were in his truck, on the road, going towards a destination. How could he, or Ray, or Craig, or the woman in the minivan have known, that they were all aiming at a single point. They were, though. Like a driver in the dark, they saw only the road in their beams, not the end of the road, not the shoulder, not the animals in the forest beside them, nor the birds, flying their migration routes asleep in the sky above.

And here he was now, on his fiftieth birthday, on his way to set things straight with his conscience. It was safe now, to say it all, to ask forgiveness. Ray was long gone, back to her country. Eddie had driven her to the airport himself, her and the child. He had sat there, in the airport parking lot, looking over the blue hood of his truck at the blue cloudless sky over Tallahassee until her plane left the ground, long after it had reached cruising altitude on its way to Atlanta. In twenty-four hours she was in another world, out of the reach of anyone who might want to find her. Out of his own reach. Craig was buried at Arlington under a white cross in the section for Iraq. It was a beautiful ceremony, the first one in the morning, and there was no one there but the officials, a priest, and him and Ray, and two of Craig's mates. It was then, when they handed her the flag, Ray had collapsed under the weight of it. The flag, the finality, the child. And he caught her, and brought her home. And then so soon after, the call. Ray was in labour. When he got there she was in intensive care, the child was gone. Eddie went back down to his truck, they said they would call him when she was awake. They said it would be a long time, but he sat there, in the truck, until the phone rang, hours later.

'Revati Miller,' he said, and they took him in to see her. She was pale, under her dark skin. She was childless, and she was inconsolable.

'Eddie, I've lost him, Eddie. He was in my care, and I let him die,' she said, and Eddie was confused for a moment.

'It's not your fault,' he said, when he realized she meant the child, Craig's child.

'Ray, it was the grief, it was too much,' he said, though he doubted he was getting through to her. She had lost the only thing of Craig's she had left, and that made no sense to her, and she couldn't breathe. Eddie sat with her a long time, until she cried herself into a kind of sleep, twitching and moaning, and then he watched her for a while. His phone rang, and it was an urgent call, he had to leave at once. He found a nurse, and left a message saying he would be back.

He took his truck because there was no time to stop at the station. The dispatcher said his partner would meet him at the crime scene.

He drove the truck down to the water's edge. The minivan was half in the water. The driver was slumped over. She had long hair, and seemed young, very young. Eddie left the door open and ran over to her. He was almost waist-deep in the water, and the van was slipping further in fast. He touched her neck, though he knew she was dead. And then he heard the sound, and the movement from the back seat. He heard the undulating siren of his partner's approach. He unbuckled the carrier from the car seat and took it over to his own truck. He placed it inside behind the passenger seat, and closed the door. He did not know why then, and did not ask that question of himself now.

'Is she dead?' Carly asked as he got out of the car, and Eddie nodded yes. It was when they started looking around the car and tried to start it that they saw the little bodies in the water. Three children between the ages of six and two, as far as they could tell. They had laid them out in a row, and Carly had stood by them while Eddie vomited behind a tree.

'Go home, Eddie,' she said to him, when the team arrived, 'I'll take care of all this and the paperwork. Take the day off, I know it's been hard for you.' She gave him a hug, and then wrinkled her nose because he smelled.

He got in the truck and drove, without stopping, to Ray and Craig's house.

What would he say now, to Father Gregory?

'Forgive me, Father, for I have sinned. It has been fourteen years since my last confession. I have committed so many sins, Father, but there is one that I must confess, because if I do not, I will be buried under the weight of it.'

Two days after the story broke in the news, that a Florida woman had drowned herself and her three children in the Wakulla river, a man had come tearing into the station. Eddie had been standing right at the front desk. The man was in his thirties, skinny, black teeth, high on something, raging. When Eddie heard his first words his mouth went dry.

'Where's my baby? You fucking motherfuckers, where's my baby?'

He began to run into the station, and was easily held by two officers, and calmed down. Eddie knew exactly what he was asking. It took the rest of them two hours of questioning, but Eddie had left by then. No one was surprised that he had taken leave for personal reasons. Everyone knew, and sympathized, about Craig, and about Ray. They knew Eddie would do the right thing by his friends. Eddie was respected, but he was also loved.

Late that night, very late, Eddie left the baby in Ray's house, asleep. He put his gloves on. He wiped the baby carrier clean. He wasn't really thinking about it. He was doing things as they came to him, instinctively, listening to his gut. His gut was made of steel. Eddie parked in the woods by the station. He knew exactly where the minivan was. He knew it was open. He crawled the last few metres dragging the carrier with him. He put the carrier in the back, and did the same on the way back to his truck. He knew he was not visible to the cameras.

Eddie went back to Ray's, to feed the baby, and wait for her to be discharged from the hospital. He slept when the baby slept, on the couch, with the creature on his chest. He hoped it was healthy. He drove three towns away where he was sure they did not know him, into a place he knew had no video surveillance, to buy diapers and formula. And then Ray called from the hospital, to say he should bring her home. He did.

What would he tell the priest, he thought, and how. He took the exit off the highway, and drove through the town towards the church. The parking lot was almost empty, but he knew Father Gregory would be there, and would be pleased to see him. He parked, and sat there a while. He thought about it, what he had done wrong. What was he doing here, and what was he going to confess to, he thought. Stealing? Or was it rescuing a baby from a meth-head who was probably, by now, dead himself? Or was it Lying? He had never lied, in fact he had said nothing all these years. Why would God have put him there, in that spot, alone, to find that child, other than to save its tiny life? And the life of Ray?

The hunt for the baby had started and ended within forty-eight hours. There were divers, but that lasted a few hours, the 'gator-laden water was much too dangerous to risk for what was almost certainly a dead baby. They looked desultorily for some sign, and gave up with great alacrity when the chief called it off. Somehow someone thought to search the van again. The carrier was found. The press conference was called. The announcement was made that there had been four children not three, and that the body would in all likelihood never be found. 'Gators were never mentioned.

That was it, Eddie thought. That was the one thing he felt bad about. He had let the 'gators take the blame.

He smiled, and he turned the key. The truck started, a smooth and lovely vibration that would be with him all the way home.

viii

Ghostrunner

You shall not bear false witness.

He could still run, Ysidro. He had run so far and so long, from his childhood, his homeland, his family, from love. He had run from war and fear and illness and malevolence and ill intent. There had been fellow runners alongside him through the years. Actual runners, but also companions in a hard-lived life. That's how he saw them all. They were all, and we are all, runners. We run through the daytime of our lives, and then we run in eternal night. He had done so many things, he thought, as he sipped his tea and looked at the mountain ridge. He had arrived there in the valley many years ago, and he knew that this was where he would be now, this was where he would end his days.

His first job in this country he had created pungent

fragrant mounds of white onions with the drumbeat of his knife. He ran in the streets at night after the day's work at the little restaurant kitchen. He was certain people could smell him running past their houses, so infused was the onion into his blood and breath. His bedclothes smelled of stale onion, and his hair and clothes. He gave up the job in a few months even though the pay was good and the timings allowed him time to run for hours each day. He explained to the lovely, large woman who owned the place that he simply could not take it any longer.

'I could think about asking you to have a cup of coffee with me,' he said, 'if I had any confidence that I could take you to my bed and not have you gag at the smell of me.'

She had smiled and said she understood, and she had asked if he would like some other job, but he had refused. It was time to move. He had run the streets and trails and his feet knew every last step within a twenty-mile radius of the town. And someone had told him of a peach harvest in Georgia, and he had packed his few things into his pick-up and left. He had headed east, stopping only to do odd jobs at farms and homes, for food, and gas money. He wondered, passing through rundown towns and abandoned gas stations, what was happening to the country and its people. Something was changing, but he did not know what it was. Torn flags, the individual stripes, red and white, flying apart from each other, were omens, a sign of something, of the world coming apart. If only everyone would run on the earth, feel the ground on their soles, on their souls, they could heal the earth, he thought. But that was then, and this was now, and he was so much older, and he had no time left to heal the world, or even himself. Everything had come apart in those years, slowly and so quietly that no one noticed except those who were caught up and flung like so many torn up pieces of paper on the careless wind of greed. No one noticed, and the land, more neon-bright and electric loud, grew ever poorer in health and spirit and humanity. The sound and light of cities, repetitive and designed to shut out the delicate senses, had done their job. Everyone had a car, and fries to eat while they drove them. But the cars were not what they used to be, friendly metal rooms that fit your life and personality. They were all the same now, reliable, ugly, smelling of plastic and esters engineered to numb. They drank gas and slid smoothly along roads made for them, cheap thin packaging for the cheap humans they transported. The fries came from kiosks on the smooth roads, made from potatoes which had never felt a human hand on them. And so it was that the old roads of his youth were littered with abandoned homes and gas stations. And there were no more little restaurants where a tired waitress in her own sweaty dress set down a plate of fries made from potatoes unevenly cut by a hungover cook. A welcome little cockroach floated in the lard, and Ysidro looked up to tell her, but he saw the curve of her breast under the ketchup stain and her tired hand pushing back her tired hair, and he wiped away the roach and ate his fries. He didn't have the money for a big tip, or any tip, but she smiled at him anyway as he walked out. Maybe it was the copper smooth skin sliding over the twisted muscle ropes of his runner's body, or maybe his long hair that followed him like a floating nest of snakes, or maybe she saw the little roach on the paper napkin and was grateful. She was surely gone from there when the traffic went to the highway and custom died down and the restaurant closed forever. He only hoped she had found somewhere better to be, and someone to be there with.

He understood now, what he had seen and felt happening then. The world was changing, and no one could have done a damned thing about it. And now it was too late. It had been too late then, but he was younger, and he had held on to the stupid hope of youth. Still, hope dies last, so he had thought about change, about running the world pure and clean and new again. He had even tried, willing, meditating on it as he ran each day, but he was just one runner, and the world was too big and change too fast for him to reverse alone. And here he was, alone with the snakes in the valley where he had once lived with a woman and children and other families. They were gone, the people, gone to find their own cars and fries and highway commutes and men with more money and power than he had. The people had gone. The snakes were still there, he had seen one just that morning.

That day, like so many of the ones before it, Ysidro rocked in his chair, and his tea slipped up to the rim of his cup and back down. The sun arrived for him in bright daylight, there at the bottom of the valley. Sharp against the sky, he saw the runner on the ridge. Gait like a wolf, hair, though not very long, lilting like a laugh on the wind. No bounce in the run. Glide. Ysidro thought perhaps he was having a stroke, dying, dead already, and the runner was none but himself, his inner self, his soul, young again, freed from the old body, running the ridges and valleys as he had done most of his life, and would do now forever. Then the runner faced into the light, his brown body caught the sun full, his red shorts were nothing like anything Ysidro had ever owned. Relief, regret, relief. He was not dying, he would not become a ghostrunner, he would live today, and tomorrow too, perhaps. He drank his tea, the runner descended the ridge and out of his sight.

Yes, Ysidro could still run. And so could the boy on the ridge, or he would not be up on that particular ridge. Ysidro didn't think he would see him again. Some ambitious kid tried that trail every once in a while, it had become more of a badge, a thing to brag about having done once, than a sustainable habit. Ysidro's Run they called it. He had been photographed for the local newspaper when famous out-of-towners came in to attempt the trail, and sought out Ysidro himself, the man who had run all the way from the ravine and up the mountain and down into the town to tell the fire chief that a fire was coming, and fast. Like a modern-day Pheidippides. He had saved the town. So Ysidro's Run it was, thirty-six miles of runner hell, or heaven, depending on what sort of runner you were.

The boy was back on the ridge in the morning, and Ysidro watched him with pleasure, because it was a beautiful stride, and because he had only a few minutes before the runner vanished into the rising sun. Ysidro decided he would climb up and take a closer look the next day. The runner may not be back, but he could do with the walk, and that night he put a shirt on the chair by his bed before he slept, so he would remember to put it on when he went. Just in case, he thought, he didn't want to scare the boy. The scars on his body scared most people, and he didn't want to scare a runner, because he was likely to take off running even faster. Morning came, and Ysidro overslept, and he rushed out and found himself halfway up the mountainside before he realized he had forgotten the shirt, it would be hanging on the back of his chair when he returned.

The boy was shirtless too, Ysidro could see him on the path ahead, too far for him to catch. He had that easy stride of a person who was made to run, to whom running came easier than walking did. It was a smooth forward motion, effortless-looking because it was effortless.

This boy may never win a race, Ysidro thought, or a medal, or be famous. But he was a runner. Ysidro realized he *was* seeing himself, a version of himself, on the trail ahead of him. He was running to catch up, and then he smiled and gave up. He could never catch up with his young self. He was still fast, and could run endlessly, but that boy was decades younger. He was *fleet.* A young Jesus, with winged feet. Ysidro liked the image. Himself, chasing his younger self, both embodiments of Jesus. The boy was beginning to diminish and Ysidro picked up his pace slightly. He was certain that he couldn't catch the younger runner, but he did want to watch him take the long downhill. There were few runners who could run downhill fast— that took a rare combination of skill, recklessness and confidence. Ysidro reached the outcrop of black rock just as the boy got to the turn where Ysidro could watch him. He sat down on the rock. What he saw took his breath away. There was no hesitation. The boy literally plummeted like a rolling rock down the steep gravelly incline. Ysidro realized a few seconds after the boy was gone from sight that his own mouth was open. He stayed on the rock for a while, contemplating what he had witnessed. When the morning sun got too hot he got up and began to run home. He kept getting the urge to shake his head in wonder, and smile.

Ysidro took a quick shower and ate the leftover stew from his dinner, and was putting on his sandals on his way out when he caught up with his own plans. They had been brewing in his head the whole time. He would do some grocery shopping in town, and then go to the school and see if he could talk to Rocha about the boy. Surely, he thought, the school coach would know him even if he wasn't in that school. Ysidro was eager suddenly, to go into the world of people. He didn't usually go into town until it was a dire necessity—until he had run out of everything. But this day he wanted to go, to find out more about the only runner in a decade to have run on the ridge three times in three days.

The pick-up complained and whined and shuddered painfully. It was long past its last days, but so was Ysidro. He just wanted it to outlast him, because there was no way he could afford another truck. But start up it did, and made it all the twenty or so miles into town without further trouble. Ysidro intended to stop at the gas station on the way back. But he saw Cenq's car in its spot and drove in so he could catch up with his friend.

'Oh man, man, man,' Cenq came out from behind the counter to hug Ysidro. 'It's been a month, and I was thinking just this morning I'd come up and see if you were alive and running. Good to see you. Come round back with me, let's have a tea.'

Ysidro just smiled, and followed Cenq into the back room where a pot of tea was ready in Cenq's self-made tea machine. They took their cups and went outside to sit under a once-red umbrella in two mismatched lounge chairs. The two men went back a long time, from when they were uneasy refugees, viewed with suspicion and thrown together unwillingly at first, but soon close friends. They had seen wives die and leave, Cenq's children grow up and leave, hard times come and go. Cenq was once the lowliest of employees at the gas station he now owned. The previous owner sold him the stock and handed over the deed because nobody came there, and he could neither stand it nor afford to stay. Cenq had gotten lucky. Here, at the border between two dry western states, a software company relocated from California. Then a spa opened. What was a one-gas station junction was now a town, with a Walmart, no less. And three schools, and a smaller campus of the state university. Students were gold to a gas station store. They came to Cenq for candy, cigarettes, chips, condoms, Corona—all their lives' basic necessities.

Ysidro enjoyed Cenq's delicious tea. They didn't talk

much, or ever reminisce. He accepted Cenq's invitation to dinner the next weekend. Then he said goodbye, paid Cenq cash for gas, and went out. He filled up his tank, checked his tyre pressure, and drove up the road to the grocery store. He didn't like going to the big chain store, and thankfully the local store, though struggling, was still in business. People still shopped there, for the local produce, homemade food and soap, sometimes even art from the university students. Ysidro suddenly had the urge to eat a samosa, though he was quite full from his stew. At this store too, he was greeted with delight and relief. People always thought he was dead, or at least lying at the bottom of the canyon with a broken leg, dying, if he didn't come in for more than a week.

Mrs Singh was there to deliver just-made samosas. She was strangely overjoyed to see him, and explained herself as she gave him two hot samosas in a small paper plate. He took a large bite leaving only a little triangle of pastry between his fingers, and he stuffed that in his mouth too.

'I wanted to talk to you, you should get a cell phone. I asked everyone how to find you.' Mrs Singh's old face was alight with excitement.

'My grandson, the youngest one,' she said, 'he starts to run, up in the mountains, just like you,' she said, 'I'm very proud, but I worry. I wanted to ask you, are they good, the samosas, have one more? I wanted to ask you if you would run with him.'

Ysidro thought about coincidence and what it meant. Here it was again, and as with every time in his life that he had been confronted with small and large moments of serendipity, he knew that this time too, the meaning would surpass his expectations. He crossed himself, and Mrs Singh shook her head and laughed.

'Oh come on,' she said, 'it's not that bad? My samosa?'

'Oh no, I didn't mean it like that. Actually, the samosas are really so good,' he said, through his mouthful of hot samosa, laughing too. 'I saw him this morning, up on my ridge. I thought I would talk to him, because—well—anyhow. I came down just to talk to Rocha, to see if he knew who the runner on the hill was, and now here you are telling me about him. I didn't know he had even started walking yet, and now you tell me he's running, on the mountain. So isn't that the work of God? He did send me to you today, don't you think?'

'Yes, either your God or mine, Ysidro,' Mrs Singh laughed, shaking and bobbing her head as she always did. He agreed he would run with the boy, of course, and told Mrs Singh to send him to his house the next day, a Saturday. Then he did his shopping, and was done. He wondered if he should talk to Rocha anyway since he was in town, decided not to, and bought himself some discounted frozen pork. On his way out he asked

Mrs Singh, who was still hovering over her samosa display, what the boy's name was.

'Karan,' she called out.

'Current? That's perfect—he does run like lightning on the mountain,' Ysidro called back. The bells on the door rang louder than her words, and he didn't catch them, but he saw her nodding and shaking her head, and he waved and left. What an odd name, he thought, probably something in a different language. Still, he liked it.

The drive back was quicker than usual that day, because there were good songs on the radio. He fell asleep after he put away his shopping, contact and communication usually exhausted him. After what he thought was about an hour, he awoke. He made himself a pipe and smoked it on the rocking chair outside, listening to a classical station on the radio. They were playing a melancholy adagio, and he thought he saw a runner on the ridge again, but he had fallen asleep on the chair, and when he woke up because of a feverish thirst he wasn't sure if it was a dream or if the boy had been running on the ridge. He ate a quick dinner and fell asleep again, this time reading in his bed. In the morning there was a knocking on his door, and he smiled as he went to open it. The boy stood there, Current, already shining wet from the run straight up the hill and then down to the house, in his red shorts and a pair of shoes—they were brown, all shoes were brown after a few minutes on the mountain.

'Mr Ysidro,' he said hesitantly, 'my grandmother said,' and then he just stopped, and smiled. He was older than Ysidro had thought he would be. And thinner and taller too. But close up he was more a runner than anything else at all, and Ysidro invited him inside to wait while he got some coffee and some shoes on.

'I've only been up a few minutes,' he said, 'I can't run without my coffee.' He picked up the cup and drank the coffee down, and slipped his feet into his shoes. Then boy and man took off up the scrabbly slope to the ridge. The exertion and the unspoken competition was exhilarating to them both, and they laughed when they reached the top. Then they settled into that rhythmic forward motion of a long-distance runner who knows he never needs to stop, who knows he can run forever till the circle of light sinks in front of him and another comes up to his back. They didn't say much to each other at first, Ysidro and Karan. After a while, though, Karan began to talk about his school, and his music class, and a certain girl, Mayra, he had asked her to go with him to prom, and she had declined.

'She said her father would kill her,' he said. 'He doesn't want her to date anyone who is not entirely white, and not entirely Christian,' he told Ysidro, laughing, but bitterness came through. Ysidro did not laugh. He knew all about that. He just let the boy talk, and talk he did. When they came down the mountain two hours after they had first met, they were friends. The boy came inside and sat down at the kitchen table. 'Do you run—your run—often?' he asked.

'No. I'm worn out. I'm sure that if I run up there as I used to I'll break my own heart,' Ysidro said smiling, in case the boy took him too seriously. 'I'm close to seventy, and I live alone up here, and you know what this run is like.' Karan said nothing, he seemed uncertain.

'But wouldn't you rather die running than just sitting here?' It came out suddenly, and he stood up, perhaps embarrassed for having said it.

'No,' Ysidro said, wanting him to stay, wanting to reassure him, 'you are right, of course. I would rather die running. When I saw you up on the ridge for the first time I thought I had died, and you were my soul, running on the ridge. I was sorry it wasn't, actually.' And then without thinking, he slipped off his soaking wet shirt. The boy gasped, and Ysidro realized his mistake. Both said nothing for a few seconds, and then both spoke at the same time, the boy apologizing for staring, Ysidro apologizing too, for everything, and for nothing. Ysidro's torso, front and back, was a mess of thin and fat welts one on top of the other, a landscape of low mountain ridges seen from far away. Except it wasn't.

It was skin muscle that had healed after being ripped open again and again, and everywhere. The scars were horrific, and anyone with the slightest imagination was reduced to trembling misery on seeing them, fearful of finding out how they came to be, hurrying to turn away.

'Please tell me what...' the boy said, and then he did something no one had ever done before. He came to Ysidro and touched his skin. Not with his fingertips. He placed his whole palm on Ysidro's side and moved it along the breadth of his torso, slowly, feeling the poor serrated flesh. Horror and sadness clouded his young face and fell in thin streams from his eyes. After a long while he seemed to come back into the moment, the house, himself, and he stepped back again, but did not apologize for his intrusion. He sat on the chair and looked at Ysidro, waiting to be told. He didn't wipe his eyes. Ysidro told him a story he had never told anyone before, not even the women who had held that same body to their own.

It was a woman, what else. Ysidro was nineteen, she was twenty-six or seven. Two children old anyhow. Married to the owner of the largest coffee plantation in the entire north of his country. They never thought of themselves as natives, these Europeans whose families had lived and taken from the land for over two centuries. They held on to their whiteness, their superiority, their foreignness. Ysidro had laid eyes on the woman all the time, every man who worked in the plantation or on the house grounds, young or old, had laid eyes on her. The story was so simple as to almost need no telling. The woman became pregnant with her third child, the child came out, and was darker than its mother and her husband, mother and child were sent away immediately. The boss looked for the perpetrator of the worst crime imaginable to him—someone had progressed from laying eyes on his property to laying hands on her. Someone had progressed from envy, from covetousness, to theft. Ysidro was tied up in a barn for six days, given nothing but water, and beaten with progressively thinner branches stripped of their leaves. Coffee.

'The first day, they started with a thing as thick as your wrist, so it bruised the muscle and bone, and they ended with a switch no thicker than your thumb, so that it cut deep into the skin and felt rough, left an imprint, in my nerves. Six days. On the seventh they rested, and so did I. I couldn't see the mess, or reach it or move well enough to put salve on it, my friends looked after me. I am grateful that it never got infected, just healed up, and the red dried up, and the blue faded, and now after all these years it's turned white. That's all, there was not much to it. Except bitterness and—well, pain. So much pain that my eyes dried up.'

After a long silence filled with the insistent scolding

of a wren, Karan asked him, 'What about the child? The woman?'

'What?' Ysidro asked, momentarily puzzled by the question. And then he laughed, startling the boy.

'It had nothing to do with me,' he said. 'Didn't you understand, it was one of the other men, or all of them, for all I know. I never had anything to do with the woman. My compatriots turned me in to the boss, they just felt I would be able to endure the beatings better than they could—I was the youngest and the strongest.' And then he smiled ruefully. 'I ran every day,' he said. 'Miles and miles and miles. And after I had healed enough, I ran from there. I ran from the plantation, the town, the state, and the whole bloody country.' The wren had stopped its chirping, and there was a real silence outside.

'I looked at the woman, all the time, I even fantasized about her. But I never touched her—I wouldn't dare,' Ysidro said. 'You know why?'

'Why?' Karan asked.

'Because, they would have done this to me,' Ysidro said, laughing, and pointing to his tortured self. Karan was shaken. After a while he stood up to go, and said he would be back the next day.

'Come after you're done. I'll make you breakfast and coffee.'

It became a routine for them. They ran together

a few times a week, and when the boy ran alone he would come down to eat with Ysidro. The summer went quickly, and Ysidro knew the boy had become stronger and faster because he dragged him hard when he could, and timed him once a week. Cross-country season would reveal Karan to the world, or at least the state's high school running world.

The songbirds were back, they had been to his home, Ysidro thought, they went every year and came back, just like that. He spread seeds for them, and envied them. They could go anywhere. And we people, he thought, we have made it so that we can go nowhere, do nothing freely anymore. How far could I run, if I left from here tomorrow morning and never stopped, he thought, if I kept on running, through days and nights. Would I make it back, to the place I came from? The place I left behind? Do I even want to go there? And that thought brought him relief, because he knew he loved it where he was, here, in this sweet valley, with Harris hawks circling overhead, his friends in the town, and now, this beautiful boy, his next generation. He had no children, but the one thing he prided himself on, he would pass on. His run. Without knowing it, like all children take their parents' essence forward into the time of the world, this boy would take his essence into the days when Ysidro was gone.

As he drove up the road lost in thought, he

was blinded by a sharp flash from metal or mirror somewhere below him. He was dazzled, and put on the brakes a little, he didn't want to end his life in a fall. It wasn't a long way down, but it wasn't worth the risk. He always thought that if he did drive off the mountain, he would rather land dead than severely injured, because there was no one to look after him. He didn't want to end his days in a hospital bed being looked after by the indifferent state. He still felt the anxiety of an outsider, he always had, and always would, even as a citizen. It was why, he supposed, he was comfortable with Cenq, or Mrs Singh, but not as much with Rocha. Cenq and Mrs Singh were different from him in every way—the countries they came from, the food they ate, their histories and lives. Even their religions. But to the majority, he, Cenq, Mrs Singh, were still, and would always be, immigrants. Not white, and so, the other. Ysidro was surprised at himself. He had never let such thoughts settle on him before. Before he could sort it out, there was the shine of metal in his eye again, and he was puzzled and curious enough about it to edge the truck to the side of the mountain. He parked and got out, crossed the dirt track, and looked down into the valley, not so far below him. A mess of devil trees had taken over every part of the land below except the road itself, but he clearly saw that the shine of metal was from a light-coloured car parked just off the road. He shrugged and was about to turn away when he heard, quite clearly, a woman, or girl, shout, once, and then again, but the second scream was cut off suddenly. He scrambled a little off the road to see if he could get a closer look. He thought the car door was open, but through the branches and trees, he wasn't sure. Then he heard the rough engine, and saw the car clearly as it took off back towards town, it was white, and was soon obscured by a cloud of red-brown dust. Ysidro went back to his truck and drove home.

And now here he was, in the courtroom, and it was full. Everyone there waited for his word. And his word, he knew as they all did, would begin or end this case, and this boy's life. The dead girl's father was there, Ysidro had heard that the mother was unconscious still, had been for weeks, since the day she had heard.

The plastic-covered Bible felt cold on his palm. Ysidro raised his other hand and said, 'I do.'

He looked at the people around him. His community. The policemen and women, the clerk, Judge Matsura squinting at him, Cenq, his face a crumpled ball of worry, the Singh family, looking blankly ahead of them, and, directly in front of Ysidro, the accused. The boy. Innocent, beautiful, running boy. Innocent. Certainty welled up in Ysidro's heart, and in his throat, and in his eyes, and he knew this was the truth. There is only one truth, he thought. And this was it. He felt it, as clearly

as he felt the sun on his shoulders when he ran. He
looked into the boy's eyes and knew he was right. He
knew it because this boy was him, and because he was
this boy. Ysidro had known it the first day he laid eyes
on him. A year ago, he thought. A year ago almost to the
day. He remembered it, like it was a very long time ago,
like some distant part of his life. His life was emptier
then, before this boy, he was older then than he was
now. He hadn't known it then, but he had given up on
expectations, on anything being any different. He was
not waiting, or wanting, just living out his days. One day
and then the next, nothing to make any one memorable.
Each day ended the same way, the next began the same
as the last. And then, one day, a year ago, one didn't.
This boy had run into his life.

'Proceed,' Judge Matsura said. He was ready to
answer the question. It was not about truth or lies, it
was not about what happened or what was done or not
done. None of that mattered. What mattered now was
that another beautiful life was not thrown away after
the one already gone.

'The boy,' he began, and the lawyer said gently, 'Use
his name, please.'

Ysidro began again. 'Karan was with me all that day,'
he said. 'We were running the long run. My run. Ysidro's
Run. So it would be impossible…'

'What time did the defendant arrive at your
residence?' the lawyer interrupted him.

'Around seven, no later than half past,' Ysidro said.

'You know this how?'

'Sunrise in my valley comes late, and the sun had already risen,' Ysidro answered. He decided to do as the lawyer had told him, prepared him. He would answer questions directly.

'What time did you leave your house to begin the run?'

'Around eight, after my coffee.'

'Where did you go?'

'Up the mountain. The starting point for the trail you all call Ysidro's Run.'

'Did you run the entire distance?'

'Yes we did.'

'How far is that?'

'Thirty-six miles.' There was a gasp around the courtroom in spite of the fact that everyone knew the distance well. Hardly anyone had run the trail, or even any of it. But there was no one there who didn't know it. Ysidro's Run accounted for more than a few percentage points of the town's business.

The questions went on, Ysidro answered them. He reconstructed a day, just not *the* day, for everyone gathered there. Everyone had seen the boy and the dead girl together, everyone knew the boy's love for the girl, everyone knew the dead girl's father and his feelings about immigrants and people who were not of his kind.

Two people knew the truth. The one who was dead and the one who killed her. And, Ysidro thought, himself. He knew the truth. And therefore, what he said here did not matter. The ultimate truth was what mattered. He crossed himself, and then he lied.

Outside, there was no one around, it was quiet, and a warm dry wind blew down the street. He walked to his truck and got in. He sat a while, eyes closed, breathing, attempting to empty his mind of all the images of the past few hours, breathing, feeling the hot steering wheel on the skin of his hands, breathing. He fell asleep. He was startled awake by the thud of a car door closing. He watched as Mr Singh helped his old mother get in. They hadn't noticed him, and Ysidro didn't say anything. The car faced into the sun, and brightness bounced off its shiny white metal into his eyes. Ysidro started up his own truck. A good stew and a full pipe waited for him at home.

ix

Heart of Gold

You shall not covet your neighbour's wife.

The little boy in the seat next to Gomes fell forward and jerked awake yet again. Gomes took his sweater out of his bag and folded it into a pillow. He rearranged the boy so he was horizontal on the seat, his legs hanging off, but his head cradled in Gomes's lap. Then Gomes put his own head against the window with the sweater pillow to protect him. He watched villages appear and be left behind with the daylight as they travelled into the night. He saw a few lights in the darkness occasionally and knew there were small huts in the farm countryside, soft brown thatched roofs among the wet green of rice fields. He smiled, he was home, in God's country. His eyes grew heavy as palm trees blurred along the roadside. His last thought as he too succumbed to a deep journey sleep was that his mother would love the Alfonso mangoes he had brought for her. There were none like those in all of Kerala.

Gomes awoke to find his lap and the seat beside him empty, and the bus empty too. They were stopped at a small terminus. He didn't know how long they had already been there, the bus driver wasn't in his seat. Gomes thought he would have time at least to use the facilities, or a tree, whichever was less crowded and cleaner, maybe even get a cup of coffee. He got up hurriedly and went outside. He saw the little boy with his mother. The mother smiled at him, and he smiled back, and felt a glow of benevolence. Visiting the toilet which was mercifully clean, getting a cup of coffee and a cigarette, and stretching his legs a bit had put him in a pleasant mood. He would enjoy the rest of the two-hour journey, one he had done many times, but not as happily as this time.

He was glad to be home. The house, all dark polished mahogany and polished shiny brass, his hands knew the warm wood of the banisters as he came down the stairs from his bedroom, his feet knew that cool stone floor of the quadrangle outside the kitchen, and the childhood within him answered as he heard his mother's voice, calling him, telling him his breakfast was on the table. Breakfast was not on the table. The white lace tablecloth was blinding in the sunlight. It was beautiful, made by one of his mother's sisters, the one he called 'Mother Superior of the Sisters of Vengeance.' Always in her crisp white sari, always making lace with the funny little seed-pod-looking thing in her dancing fingers. Hands always busy, mind always angry, mouth always sarcastic. He missed her suddenly, the old biddy. But she was gone, dead when he was a teenager, the same year he had lost his father.

In the centre of the white tablecloth, like a gift from the Magi, a pyramid of golden mangoes glowed on a golden plate. He could smell fish, and he almost laughed out loud. Fish for breakfast. What could be better. Life was so beautiful, he didn't think he could be happier, and then his mother walked in with the cook behind her, both carrying steaming bowls of curry and appams, and he was happier.

'What are you smiling about?' his mother demanded, and he smiled even more, because he was there, and he was alive.

'Because I'm alive,' he said. She shook her head. This child of hers had always been a bit odd, but he was smiling, and she had never seen him like that before, uncomplaining, cheerful even, and now, he couldn't stop smiling.

'Has something happened? Anthony?'

'Hmm, yes,' he said. After church, he thought. After he had talked to the new priest. The one who didn't know him. After he had confessed to God. After that, he would confess to his mother.

His mother knew him well, and left well alone for the moment. She knew he would tell her eventually, and she knew he had something to tell. As a little boy secrets seemed to fill him up, make him physically uncomfortable. He tried hard to stuff them down, but they just bubbled out of him. He would tell her, after making sure she would never tell anyone else. He would tell her where he had hidden his ball so his brother would not find it, what his best friend the Khan boy had stolen from their shop, why the smartest girl in his class had failed the final exams. She watched him eat his breakfast. He tore a piece off the soft crepe and formed it into a scoop. He tried to use it like a mini ladle, and each time it collapsed into the hot orange fish gravy, and he would smile and plunge his fingers in to retrieve it and carry it carefully into his mouth. He would lick each finger after this and start over with another piece. She shook her head. The same boy she had always known. Anthony never did learn from his mistakes. He even said to her, when he was little, 'Amma, what is the point? Every moment is new, everything you do is new.' This was incredibly illogical, and she didn't know where to begin to explain to him that it would bring him nothing but trouble. She left it to life, to teach him. And asked Saint Thomas to show him the way. She wished he would stay this time. But there was nothing for him to do here, not any longer. He didn't want to live in Karuvilla and sell sundries in the shop as his father had done, he never had wanted that. So she was glad, not for herself, but for him, that the Khan boy had found him that job. It was far away, but it was a job, and her son seemed, for once, to be at peace with himself.

Gomes walked home from the church even though Father Melvin had offered to drive them both home, him and his mother. He preferred to walk. He needed to, after the big breakfast, the long sermon, the deep confession, he needed air. He said goodbye to his mother at the church steps and took off through the woods behind the church. He walked slowly under the strange mix of ancient palm and cashew trees.

Gomes was relieved that Father Mathu was no longer around, his story would have been too much. On second thought, probably not. 'Old' Father Mathu was old enough to have heard and seen everything in his long life. Gomes was glad he didn't have to endure the familiar disapproval, and yet, he missed it. The pros and cons of the absence of Father Mathu buzzed around in his head all the way to the edge of the water where he suddenly found himself.

He rolled up his pants and sat down on a dead palm trunk. He took off his shoes and put them up next to him and tucked his rolled socks into them. He let his feet touch the surface of the slow flowing water and then pushed them in, feeling the cool wet mud between his toes. He could see the rice paddies on the other side, people knee-deep, bent over working, he could hear the sound of children playing, and he was, once again, overwhelmed by gratitude for his life, and, gratitude to a certain constable who had listened to his pleas and saved his life. What could he learn, he thought, from the mistakes of his life? Or even just the recent past? What could he possibly get from the strange and singular events of the last few years, from the things he had done that had almost cost him his life, things that he would not, and could not ever do again, and not only because Asim Khan was dead twice over. Gomes knew he would never make the same mistakes again, because he would never again have the opportunity to make them.

Asim Khan was dead, and Gomes had not yet mourned his friend. They had been all of five years old when they first met, on that first day of junior school. Everyone had assumed they were twins, and exclaimed disbelievingly over how alike they looked when told they were not even related. They were seated next to each other that day because they were the only two non-Hindus in the class, and next to each other they stayed, for the rest of their lives.

'We have the same God, the same heavenly father,' Asim would say, 'Isn't that why we look so alike?' Gomes found this logic silly—based on that all men should look identical—but he had to admit it was miraculous. There were not many, other than their mothers and siblings, who could easily tell them apart.

'There is a way to tell us apart,' Asim said when they were urinating on a wall one day. 'Yours is twice the size of mine, brother,' he said, and collapsed with laughter. As they grew older, he used their startling similarity to do many nefarious things. People in their town and the villages around got to know this, so he pushed it further and further. He made Gomes take a test for him that he knew he would fail. Then a job interview. One day he asked Gomes to take his mother shopping. He told Gomes to pretend he had a toothache so he wouldn't have to speak, because then for sure she would know he was not her son. While Gomes wandered in the market with Asim's mother, Asim robbed a store in the neighbouring town. He made his own mother his alibi, and she easily convinced the CID inspector that he couldn't have done it. Any number of shopkeepers and vendors in the market would back her up, she said. The charges were dropped, but Gomes understood and admitted to himself that his own mother was right. His dearest friend Asim Khan was a thief and a liar and a deviant. But Anthony Gomes loved him, and he had been heartbroken when, after twenty-two years of being joined at the hip with him, Asim went away to Mumbai to work for one Mushtaq Bhai, a distant uncle on his mother's side.

Gomes didn't have much time to miss him though. Asim came back every few months, laden with expensive gifts for his own family as well as the Gomes family. At first Gomes was overjoyed. He was happy for his friend's growing success. Each time Asim was better dressed, his presents more opulent. But after the fourth or fifth visit, Gomes' enthusiasm began to pall. It may even have been as early as the third. Asim spoke too loudly, his clothes were too shiny, he wore too many rings, he had wads of money to throw down at the only restaurant close to them. And then, three years ago almost to the day—Asim came back and announced to all who would listen that he was married. He produced cherry red photo albums full of the proof, of the nikah and the very fancy party after. While turning the pages he boasted loudly and endlessly about his new wife's incredible beauty and cooking skills. Gomes smiled to himself as he thought about that conversation. Asim had told the truth about her beauty, and had lied about her cooking skills. No, Asim had not lied about her beauty. Shahnaz had abundant breasts, the most divine thighs that Gomes had ever imagined a woman having, her lips, he could have lived in those lips for the rest of his life. And the way she moved, he could hardly ever contain himself long enough to satisfy her. She was shy and sweet and smelled like his Amma's tapioca pudding, and even tasted a bit like it. But her cooking, that was a disaster. Gomes felt his throat closing up. He loved her, that Shahnaz. His wife once, and now never to be again. It was done, all that. He had made it out by the skin of his teeth, and with his life. But God, how would he live now, forever without the touch of those hands, without that fragrant hair in his face as he did the most beautiful thing he had ever done? No, this train of thought had to stop. But he allowed himself the pleasure of the thought, and in the gloom at the river's edge, allowed too, the logical inevitable conclusion to that thought.

Gomes had looked carefully at Asim's wedding photos to find his wife's face, but in most of them it was covered in veils and jewels and flowers and he could see nothing. He took Asim's word for it. That night, the night before he was to leave, Asim was hit by a car. He was found the next day, dead in a ditch on the roadside. Gomes remembered the shock, clearly and precisely, as if it had been deeply carved into his mind somewhere, as if he was feeling it with his fingertip. Still sharp at the edges, the pain of losing his oldest dearest friend. He mourned the friend Asim had been, before he went away, before the satin shirts and gold watch and patent shoes, before the haircut and the cologne, before the marvellous gold chain that nestled in the hair on his chest. Gomes had looked at himself in the mirror that night, probably as Asim fell dead into the earth, and imagined that chain resting on his own chest. It was easy to do, because looking at Asim was like looking in a mirror anyway. He saw it all the time, his own face above a cobalt satin shirt, his own hair cut that way, his own skin smelling like Asim's, a strong manly smell that made Gomes' heart beat faster. He had thought about her, Shahnaz. She must love this smell, he had thought. She must have it on her own skin too, from her proximity, from her intimacy with her husband. And then, where had the idea come from, that vile, incredible idea? From a desire to have everything Asim had, including Shahnaz? Was it that? Or was it even bigger, stranger than that? Was it, he thought, that he wanted to *be* Asim, that he had, since that first day he met him, wanted to be Asim?

The day after Asim Khan had been buried and mourned, Anthony Gomes had told his own mother that his friend had found him a job. In Mumbai. That Asim had, in fact, returned to tell him about it. Then he had gone to Asim's house and told Asim's shocked, grieving mother that he would travel to the city and deliver the terrible news to Asim's wife. Until he actually saw Shahnaz his intentions were still good, still honourable. It must have been Shahnaz then, who made him do what he did. It was she, and her wicked desire to pretend her husband was not dead. It was she, when he stood at her door, who threw herself into his arms, who was so delighted to see him, who dragged him to her bed, who undressed him, who must have known, he thought with some shock, when she saw his erect nakedness, that he was not Asim. Size notwithstanding, there was the other obvious reason. And then, along with his very first ejaculation into a woman's body, his strange hidden thoughts, desires, intentions—came to life, and became life. Anthony Gomes ceased to exist, and Asimullah Khan came back from the dead.

For three years he lived with Shahnaz. For three years she called him by her dead husband's name, and for three years he answered to it, whether it was to go to the table to face the awful meals she cooked, to open a jar for her, to see the pigeons on the roof of the building across the road from theirs, to satisfy her never-ending desire for him with his for her. For those years, every single day, and sometimes twice and sometimes thrice each day he would take her to bed, or she would take him. The thought of it began to hurt him again, and this time it was not in his sex that he felt the loss, but in his heart, and this time it was his eyes that spilled over.

The morning after the first unbelievable night with her he was woken up by a hand shaking his shoulder. He remembered how confused he had been in that room, with the huge wooden four-poster bed, the tiles on the floor, the strange angle of the sunshine coming in through long curtains on a large barred window. And then he knew, and before he could smile, he saw a young man's face looking at him.

'Asimbhai, your wife has made you tea,' the man said. Gomes sat up hurriedly and tried to cover his nakedness. The man had laughed and said, 'Oh, are you suddenly concerned now that I will be jealous?'

That was Praful, Gomes learned. Praful, whether he knew the truth or not, never once alluded to any mischief. Praful was his right and left hand, his secretary, his accountant, his spy, his advisor. As the months went by, Gomes began to understand Praful and Shahnaz, and an army of boys and men and women who were his procurers, his sellers, his go-betweens for the police, for the taxi drivers and couriers, it was an endless chain of supply and demand. It was not only convenient for them all to let him be Asim Khan, it was safe, profitable, and unthinkable to do otherwise. So he *was* Asim Khan. He was driven around the city streets in a gleaming black Mercedes. The one which Gomes had heard about of course, from Asim. The driver, Ali, talked about the car to the exclusion of anything else. Gomes didn't pay much attention, he knew nothing about cars, and did not understand the letters and numbers Karim spoke about, and tried hard not to make it obvious that he didn't. If Karim suspected something amiss, Gomes did not see it. Either Asim had been as uninterested as he was, or, Karim hadn't noticed either way. They were always accompanied by Ali's brother Raheem who wore a large white flowing shirt and had a huge gun strapped to his torso that was clearly visible through the shirt.

Gomes was treated by his seemingly endless network of employees with great affection and great fear at once. Praful looked after everything, all Gomes had to do was show up and act authoritative. It was easy. He went to weddings and dinners and horse races. He cut ribbons and placed flowers on foundation stones at very minor ceremonies with small-time politicians. He was welcomed into expensive hotel rooms by aging madams with bevies of beautiful underage virgins, many of whom he unvirgined and revisited many times through those too short too few years. He always returned home to Shahnaz, and he always had something left for her.

What a life that was. But it was all over and done with now. He had returned home alive, he had confessed his sins to the priest, he was new again. He was Anthony Gomes again. His mother's boy, his father's son. And Asim Khan—well—he was dead again. Gomes wondered what they would all think, when a body never turned up. He wondered if they would finally find Asim's hometown, or his mother. He doubted very much that they would even look. He had realized early in his life as Asim that no one knew where their boss had come from, Asim had never told anyone. In the drug business, it was best to keep secrets. It was best to have a place to run to, and hide, that absolutely no one, not even his own wife knew about.

Gomes had followed his instinct, and he had simply used Asim's train ticket to take him to the city. After that, everything had happened like clockwork. He stepped out of the station with Asim's bag. A man, who he got to know as Raheem, his personal bodyguard, immediately took his bag from him and walked him to the waiting car where he opened the door, closed it for him when he was seated, and then got in the front seat with his brother. They drove through crowded streets and what looked to Gomes like the road along the city dockyards to a building in an older part of the city. Raheem had walked up with him to the top floor, waited till Shahnaz had flung herself at Gomes, placed the bag inside the door and left, mumbling something about waiting downstairs. The flat was old but huge, and magnificent. There were velvet tapestries of Mecca and miniature replicas of golden mosques on marble-topped tables, glass and gilt everywhere, the music system that Asim had boasted about was there, and, in the bedroom, a cupboard full of flamboyant suits and ties and those satin shirts and kurtas and gold bracelets and yes, several gold chains to choose from, and shoes—so many pairs that he could wear a different one every day of the week and not have worn the same one for months. He had heard about all this from Asim, of course, and at first dismissed it as lies, and then, every subsequent visit, he had believed more and more. When Asim gave him a gold watch, when he brought him a silk shirt, when he brought him a dozen underpants in some kind of material he didn't know existed, Gomes had finally understood that everything was true. He had to accept that Asim Khan, his criminal friend, was a rich man living in luxury.

A child screamed across the river, and Gomes had a moment of disorientation. Was he a child again, waiting for Asim to come find him, there at the river's edge, where everything had come to an end? This was the end, he knew, and there was no going back. He had confessed to sins he hadn't known existed three years ago, he had repented and he had asked forgiveness, from God, from those he had sinned against who didn't even know it, from the young priest, who, Gomes thought, must have been pretty addled by his story. But even the priest agreed that God had shown him a way back by bringing him home, alive. All Gomes must do now was take it. Leave everything behind and take this path. Leave behind that life, that woman, the man he had attempted to be, and be the man he was born to be. Yet again, the thought of life without Shahnaz reduced Gomes to a trembling terror, and yet again, he forced thoughts of her away.

If it hadn't been for that constable, Eapen, he would be dead anyway. He would be without Shahnaz anyway, burning in hell. But the constable had listened to his pleas, and taken him to the hospital, and had waited while he was treated. The doctor told him Eapen had left only when he had been assured that the man he had brought in, poisoned and near death, would live, and live undamaged. Gomes owed that man his life, and vowed never to forget it. Who had poisoned him, he wondered. It was one of the other men at that meeting, certainly. All of them wanted Asim Khan dead, and now they had their wish. They could have his turf, they could have his women and his sources and his pushers and even his car. But Shahnaz—what would happen to her? Anthony Gomes stood up then and rinsed his feet in the water. He wiped them as best he could on the grass and put his socks and shoes on. Then he ran all the way home. He ran into the house calling to his mother. He sat her down and sat by her feet. He told her of his journey into the life of Asim Khan, about his lies, his deceptions, his sins and troubles, and of course, his beloved, beautiful wife. And then he told her of his death, and his rebirth. Then he put his head in her lap, and, though she made no move to touch or comfort him, he sobbed his heart out.

'God will punish you in his own way,' she said finally, when he was done. He got up and sat beside her.

'But are you not angry?' he asked, and she, to his

absolute amazement, smiled at him. She had an odd calm about her.

'My dear little Thona,' she said, using a name for him that she had not since he had begun to walk, 'how can I be angry? You say I have a daughter-in-law. Will you not bring her to me?'

Gomes nearly cried all over again. 'No,' he said to his mother, 'she was not my wife, Amma. She was his. I deceived her. I played a game, and I lost. I can never see her again.' His mother tried to speak but he stopped her with a shake of his head.

'I have talked to Father Melvin. Amma, I will join the Society of Jesus as a novice. I will be a priest, Amma.'

There was a moment of silence. Then his mother began to laugh. Gomes was startled, but he neither showed it nor did he ask what she had found amusing. He knew she would tell him.

'My sister always said you should be a priest,' she said. 'You know, your favourite aunt. Mother Superior of the Sisters of Vengeance. I always told her she was crazy. That you of all people didn't have it in you. But she must be laughing down at us now. Well, Anthony, if that is what you want. But sleep on it, and tell me how you feel tomorrow. Will you do that?'

'Yes,' he said, and they went to eat dinner, and spoke no more about it.

～

Inspector Eapen leaned close to his wife and whispered in her ear, 'Isn't this the best wedding ever, my dear, isn't it?'

The tables were full of happy young people from his daughter's class, her friends and their families, her brand new husband's friends and families, all Eapen's own colleagues from constables to the chief inspector and their wives and children, everyone seemed to be smiling and talking and eating at the same time. The food was absolutely glorious. Biryanis and roast chicken, chilli roast beef and fried fish, and the cake—he had never tasted anything that made him think it was food for the gods. The cake was definitely was.

'Who is that man with that—that—that creature?' his wife said to him, pointing discreetly at his old friend, Anthony Gomes. Eapen laughed. Shahnaz was a creature, her beauty did leave people without words.

'That's Anthony Gomes,' Eapen said. 'And that beautiful woman by his side, that's his wife.'

'Oh my God, that's Gomes? The one who sends us Diwali sweets every year? Because you saved his life a hundred years ago, *that* Gomes?'

'That Gomes. I really want to know what happened in his life, or at least that day, when he was near death, in the cell. They thought he was drunk, when they brought him in. I was the only one in the whole station who believed him, thank God, or he would really have died. I know someone tried to kill him. He's never told me, and I doubt he ever will, who, and why. I'll keep asking, though.' Eapen didn't say it to his wife, but he had always thought the whole thing had something to do with Shahnaz. Gomes had been married to her as long as Eapen had known him, and it was an uncharitable thought, Eapen knew, but he couldn't help it—he always wondered how and why this angel had married Gomes. 'This cake is just perfect,' his wife said, and Eapen sighed. It was the best day of his life, he thought, and he had no savings left. But everyone was so happy. The band began to play again, and it was his favourite song. He stood up and faced his wife.

'Can I have this dance?' he said, and she took his hand and they joined the only other couple on the dance floor, Anthony Gomes and his wife, Shahnaz. If Eapen could read minds, he would have known the reason for Gomes' brilliant smile. Gomes was thinking about his mother, the morning after he had confessed to her. 'Thona,' she had said, 'You will never be a priest, I told my silly sister that when you were five years old.' She had been right, of course. She had also been a wonderful mother-in-law to Shahnaz, who had found him, somehow, and arrived at their doorstep, heavy with his mother's grandchild. Gomes was smiling because he could see that grandchild, now affectionately known as Doctor 'Saint' Francis, eating cake and shaking his head at his parents' public romance. Gomes was smiling, because the wine and the circumstance had shaken loose the love, and the silly sentimentality that he carefully contained in his heart, and it had overflowed into his veins, and onto his face, where Eapen saw it.

Eapen smiled back at Gomes as they passed each other.

'I'm a miner for a heart of gold,' he sang out loud. Yes, and they were getting old, Eapen thought, him and Anthony Gomes.

x

Elegy in a City Churchyard

You shall not covet your neighbour's goods.

Ignacio Battista had lived in the churchyard my whole
memory. My mother said he had lived there since before
she and my father had moved there, and Derya, whose
family owned the Turkish bakery on the Wilhelmplatz,
said her father said he had been there since they came
over from Turkey. I didn't doubt that, he was old, close
to a hundred probably. I didn't pay that much attention
to him nowadays, I hardly ever even walked past the
church, I was usually on my bicycle, so Ignacio Battista,
the church, the shops, the market, the street, the trees,
summers, autumns, winters, I whizzed past everything
without seeing much. I only thought of him because he
had brought the street to a halt that day. I was forced to
stop and disembark. I stood there with the bike between

my legs, outside the church wall, watching with the rest of my neighbourhood. There was a policewoman among the small crowd, I wondered if she had been summoned or was just there, part of the audience. There was no reason for the law to be there anyway, it was just Ignacio Battista yelling, with pauses to clear his throat and spit great gobs of his battered old lungs out.

'At least he's yelling in German now,' Derya said to me, and when I looked puzzled she said, 'He used to yell in Portuguese, and no one knew what he was on about, so by the time someone found someone who could translate...' then she just shook her head.

We listened for a while, and it turned out that he was angry at the neighbourhood for having put a big umbrella in his compound, apparently he was highly insulted that someone had thought he might need protection from the very wet weather we'd been having these last weeks.

'Am I a child?' he asked the crowd, and some of them were smiling and nodding, and someone said 'yes,' which made him even angrier.

'I am ninety-four years old, how do you think I managed, without you people, you were not born when I was having the worst days of my life.'

The crowd smiled and someone murmured, 'Were you all alone in the city then?'

He turned toward the voice, and I was struck by

how long it had been since I had really looked at him. I used to walk slowly by the church, because I always hoped to catch a glimpse of him. I don't remember when I became aware of my fascination for him. I must have just started to walk out on my own. Not when I first learned to walk—though I'm sure my mother or father would push me past him in my stroller—but when I actually walked. So I could have been four, or even three. I remember my father being so proud when I first said the old chap's name correctly.

'Ignacio Battista,' I said, and my father laughed his rich happy laugh and told me I was the cleverest boy in the world.

'A linguist,' he said proudly to my mother, who shook her head and sighed. The professions my father thought up for me were strange and diverse, and there was a new one each week depending on what I had achieved on that day of my boyhood. She could have pointed out to him that my fluency in Tamil and English and German hadn't impressed him, whereas my being able to say Ignacio Battista apparently did. But she just rolled her eyes.

Ignacio had always had a beard. I had somehow missed the progression of black to white. I had seen him, talked to him, known him almost every day, I hadn't noticed. But my memory placed the younger man next to the man shouting at the crowd. It shocked

me now, that image of him. He must have been close
to seventy even then. He was a big muscular man with
a pointed black beard, smooth cheeks and forehead, a
long-sleeved white shirt with the sleeves neatly rolled
like envelopes up over his elbows, his hair, black as
his beard flaring away from his temples in one straight
long sweep, was shiny like one of my vinyls. He had
large white teeth, they shone in his smile, which was,
at least for me, at least back then, frequent. He was
not so big now. Of course it was because I was smaller
then, but he really was much bigger. His white shirt was
still white, but I could see the frayed strands where the
sleeves had been torn off, the buttons seemed stitched
closed, his skin was visible through the transparency
of the worn fabric. His hair floated in a puff like steam,
a halo, over his scalp, as if it had lost its weight and
desire to acquiesce to gravity. In fact, the whole man
looked that way—insubstantial. A rock, a tree trunk, a
great ship—those were the words that came to mind
when I thought of him, the Ignacio of my childhood,
and my teens.

He was still pacing up and down, but not with as
much energy. The crowd dissipated, the police lady
encouraged them to move along, and Ignacio went
back to his beautiful antique cane lounge chair which
was now protected from the elements by a very large
canvas garden umbrella. I watched him lean his head

back and close his eyes. I took off then, I was already late for work. The day got hectic fast, two of my staff were off for 'personal reasons,' I had to wait tables and when it got a bit crowded during the afternoon I even made a burger and fries for a customer. That evening as I washed up and locked up I thought about him again, Ignacio. He had been a fixture in my life. A fixed point in my universe, without my ever seeing it that way, until now. I had had a relationship with him that changed every half decade of my own three or so. I wondered now if that saying of his name evoked some kind of magic that tied him to me. I wondered if he remembered my name. It made me sad, to think he might not.

I was walking with—what was her name, the person I had a crush on in my first real school year—those years when I didn't know there were supposed to be sexes and I belonged to one and my crushes had to belong to the other one, but Sami—that was their name—didn't belong to any sex, gender, not yet, not then anyway. I was walking with Sami, waiting for her, him, them, to talk. I never struggled then to think about him or her, language fouls up your mouth and your mind, and people get pronouned and raced and sexed, and by the time you are seven or eight, or maybe even five, you don't know which way is up anymore, or that people are people, not social units. Anyway, Sami, the love of my young life, decided to walk through Ignacio's compound. It was the church compound, I didn't know this was not a good idea. Sami obviously knew, and before I knew what was happening we were running away from Ignacio who was yelling and running after us. We stopped right outside the wall, Sami knew he couldn't come past that invisible line. Like a bridge troll, he was stuck there. Sami handed me an apple from the bag she had stolen as she ran through Ignacio's space. Sami was a liar and a thief, and I'd got away easy. It could have turned into heartbreak and a criminal record, but, she, he, Sami, left that year, and my crush dissipated like a rotten smell.

When the powers that be decided I was good enough for college I was moved to the level one school. I took it all very seriously from then on, the school work, my parents, the relationships I had, the clothes I wore. That was the year I really spoke with Ignacio. He wasn't crazy at all, I'd seen him talking with my parents enough times, and other people too, I'd seen him sweeping his yard, repairing his chairs and chests of drawers, even polishing his black leather boots. He smiled at me almost every day when I walked past him, and sometimes waved, and one day called me into the yard.

'Do you like to read?' he asked me, and I said yes, of course I did. He took me to a shelf he had standing against the church wall. He had several odd bits of furniture under the trees, with plastic tarp neatly and carefully covering it all. I took his life for granted, as did everyone in that area of the city. We, or at least I, never thought it strange or unusual that a grown man lived outdoors in a churchyard, that he slept and cooked and ate there, that he read and I learned later, wrote there, and occasionally showered in the church bathroom.

One year *Stern* magazine sent a reporter and a photographer to do a story on him, and that year we all looked at Ignacio with a bit of curiosity. It happens when you have to show a tourist your city, I suppose, like when my father's family came from Chennai and I took my cousins to see the cathedral. We climbed up into one of the spires up the old stone spiral, up and up and up, and each flight I looked out at my city through the portals in the stone, past the angels and saints and gargoyles, out on the courtyard, down on the Rhine, and I promised myself I would do that more often but I never did it again. When Ignacio was featured in *Stern*, I read the article again and again, and looked at those photos of Ignacio now and Ignacio as a boy, and a young man, the journalist had found them in the archives. There was even a photo of him as a baby in his father's arms, taken right in front of the church, the church where he now lived. That article answered questions I had never had, and had therefore never asked. And, like the cathedral, I promised myself I would spend more time with Ignacio, ask him about his life, and how he came to live there, in the churchyard. I knew after reading about it, but I wanted to hear it from him, in his own words, in his voice.

I give myself credit for having tried. I asked him, that day when he asked me to come over to him, when he asked if I liked to read. He gave me a comic book that day. I was disappointed, that was not really my thing. I asked him, though I was a little nervous, about himself.

'I saw the article,' I started, my voice a bit shaky, 'in *Stern*, it was very interesting.' He gave me a look that shut me up. I said thank you for the comic and picked up my schoolbag.

'Those people will believe anything,' he said. I put the bag back down.

'I told them my father built this church,' he said, 'I told them that my mother died because she came to see him one day with his lunch, and couldn't find him, so she climbed up the half-finished building and slipped and fell, and was impaled on an angel's wing.'

He began to laugh. And then he told me something else. After that day, I had precious information about Ignacio that no one else had, no one else knew who he was or what he had done, but me. Of course I found out that that was all fabricated nonsense too, but for years, for two decades, I thought I had the keys to his kingdom. As I rode past his church that night, I wondered if he remembered all he had told me, or if it was gone, like everything else in his mind.

'Do you read the newspapers too?' he had asked me, and before I could answer, he said, 'No, you weren't born then. How old are you?'

'Fourteen,' I told him.

'Fourteen? Has it been that long? You were a baby when your father would walk around here with you, we'd talk, him and I, where is he, what's he doing?'

'He got hurt. He hurt his back. He can't walk now, my mother takes him out in a wheelchair,' I said, 'but maybe she doesn't bring him this way—she takes him to the Flora, he likes to look at the plants and trees you know, and they drink tea there every afternoon.' I was babbling a bit, nervous, but he was kind.

'I am sorry, about your father, he's a good man. How did it happen?'

I told him, the stairs, the fall, the slow realization that he would not recover. It was nothing dramatic, a simple domestic accident, but it changed our small family. It was slow too, and undramatic, the understanding that I would always live with my parents, or, they with me. I had never minded the idea. I went on trips often, to cooking conventions, restaurateur and entrepreneur conferences, my café was recommended in travel guides and shows even if it wasn't a 'must do.' I valued local clientele more than tourists in any case, I knew what it meant to have people come back again and again rather than those one-offs. Besides, tourists were seasonal. I had never told Ignacio what my café was called. I'd tell him, I thought that night as I got to bed. I'd go over there and tell him on Monday, when the café was closed. We became friends that year, my fourteenth year, when I went over there every week, to his weird living space. I enjoyed it. It was all neat and tidy, his living room was under the big beech tree, it was very cool in its vast leafy shade in the summer, magpies walked around underneath cackling harshly as they do, as we talked, me on the ground and Ignacio in his antique wood-framed cane chair. That was the year he told me, his secret, and for so many years, my secret too, till I gave it up, till I abandoned the crazy ramblings of a crazy old man. I wondered suddenly, if I was wrong.

Ignacio was almost out of his thirties, he said. It was 1964. A presidential election about to happen in West Germany. Chaos and confusion, police presence, and, carnival preparations added to the mix made the city anxious and nervous. Perfect he said, for a heist. A grand theft that got lost, that slipped beneath the river of noise and gaiety and frantic energy that flowed in the streets. Ignacio and his companions, three women and two men, literally dressed as bank robbers, alongside people dressed as clowns and whores and bears and cats he said, laughing all the while he told me the story, robbed the biggest bank in Cologne, and got away with it. They were never caught, and the enormous haul of stuff was never recovered. They didn't get any money, he explained, just stuff, because they were able to get into the vaults, through a beer cellar that was owned by one of the thieves' uncles. I remember being so thrilled with the story that I almost quivered in my bed that night, thinking about the stuff they had stolen, what it might be, where it might be now. Gold, diamonds, watches, jewellery surely, and as I got older I thought there must have been artefacts perhaps, old amazing things the Nazis had stolen from Jewish families perhaps, and as I got older still, and more aware of the world, I thought there might have been stock certificates surely. Over the years I looked up the story in the library archives, I asked older people about it, it was all true, the facts were all correct, and it was entirely plausible. I wondered where the old man had hidden his share of the stuff, or if he had sold it all, or little by little, if he had spent it, slowly, all the while that he was pretending to be so poor, living, hiding, in the city churchyard, dressed as a homeless man.

I often asked him about the heist, but that was the one and only time he told me about it. I suppose I got bored with it all eventually, though I didn't stop going to see him, and talking to him about the last comic book he'd given me.

My twenties I called the hopeful period, when I was convinced there were treasures inside the church compound, and I thought incessantly about ways I could lure Ignacio away from his spot and search his belongings. I didn't know what I was looking for, but I just knew, I just knew there were priceless things there. Those were the days I took him food, which was not surprising, all the neighbours did. My family and I were not regular contributors, but as he got older, there were regulars. There was a rotation, a calendar, substitutes if someone couldn't for some reason. Ignacio got breakfast, lunch, dinner, snacks, he got his clothes laundered and repaired, he got towels and toiletries, from the very people he now insulted and railed at. He lived in fine style, if out in the open. In the winter on days that were cold he would light a nice fire, he got to sleep inside the church on snow days.

Anyone was welcome to join him at his fire, and I often did. One cold night I brought vodka, and got him drunk, very, very drunk. He went inside the church to sleep it off, as I had hoped. I took out the flashlight I had brought for the purpose and went through his things, methodically and carefully, his four trunks, his tarp-covered shelves, I had started on the various plastic bags and boxes stacked by the wall when Father Elmer came out to smoke and asked me what I was doing. I had to leave. It was around then that I began to think the stuff had to be underground. I just knew I was right this time. It explained so much. This was why he lived there, in the churchyard. This was why he couldn't leave. Perhaps he was still waiting for an opportunity to dig it all up and disappear. Or, perhaps, he had left it too late. He needed an accomplice now, because he couldn't get it done by himself. There was no way for me to dig up the churchyard without knowing where he had put the stuff. The stuff. That was how I thought of it then, stuff. It had acquired a tremendous value in my mind over the years, as I imagined how much the stuff, whatever it was, itself would have grown in value over the years, if in fact it was gold, or jewellery, or stock certificates for old German companies that were now world corporate giants.

All the cake, coffee, hints and questions didn't get me anything, and finally, in my thirties, Ignacio was in his eighties, his mind began to go. There was nothing more to it. The closest we came to saying anything was that one night I had a mad idea that Ignacio must need some company. Some real company. A woman. So I cycled down the road to the Pascha, and requested one of the lovely ladies there to come out and help me. She was delighted and highly amused by the idea of servicing a man in the churchyard. I was ready to pay her double for having to leave her workplace, but she was quite happy to follow me on her own bicycle. I told her to take her time. It was not entirely a sham on my part, I did actually think old man Ignacio could do with a bit of fun. I had seen—no, heard—him masturbate so many times through the years. It was one of the things about him that everyone was used to, and usually he did it late at night. We all knew to walk by and ignore him if we heard him groaning and shaking, it only lasted a few minutes, and no one saw the harm.

When the lady went over and talked to him, he was pleased apparently, and I heard them laughing and talking at first, and then his grunts, I didn't think he was capable of actually fucking her, but who knew what he was capable of. I used the time to move the boxes and bags away from the ground, looking underneath for some sign that there was a stuff burial below, maybe it was smooth, or just dug up, or a plank of wood or a tile that could be moved away. I found nothing, but I heard Ignacio's successful shouts, they disturbed an owl in the tree above who began to whoop along with him.

I was over it after that. I gave it up as a mad childhood, teenage, youth fantasy that had occupied me in many ways. I began to wonder if he had told me that story at all, or if I had imagined that too, after reading about the stupid robbery somewhere.

That night I was more tired than usual. I thought about going to see the old bugger, attempting to talk to him again. Everyone knew his mind was pretty much gone now, but still, there may be something left still. There was that cat he had adopted a couple of years before—he still fed it and it was a fixture in the churchyard now. Ulrike. There was an art fair, the year he got her. Artists from all over the city set up stalls and makeshift booths and sold and painted, or made jewellery and knicknacks all around the church and in part of the compound that wasn't his. I remember talking to him that day, because I took him some apple cake my mother had made. I had waited as he ate, because I had to take the plate and fork home. He had looked around and shaken his head in disgust.

'Art,' he said, 'Who needs it.' Then the cat came sidling over and rubbed his legs. There was that funny look on his face, the Mona Lisa look. I think that's what that look is anyway—a cat rubbing on your legs.

'Hello, little cat,' he said, rubbing the spots where her whiskers sprouted.

'Ulrike Meinhof's father was an art historian, did you know that?'

'No,' I said, wondering what that had to do with anything.

'Doesn't that explain everything,' he said, and burst out laughing.

'Ulrike is a nice name for you,' he told the cat. He had seemed all right then, in those few moments, so maybe he had some lucid moments still. Maybe I would go see him again, and find them. And tell him what I had named the café, because he would get a kick out of that, if he understood.

I woke early and left home early, so I could get fifteen minutes with Ignacio. There was no crowd there that morning, and no one at all on the sidewalk. It was oddly quiet, and I looked over at where he usually sat, but he wasn't there. I went around the church to the front. Father Elmer was standing outside the front door, smoking.

'Father, good morning,' I said, still astride my bicycle,

'Good morning, Matthias, are you coming inside?' he said, alluding to my load of sin.

'No, Father, not today. Where is Ignacio?'

'Asleep inside,' he said, 'it was a little too cold for him last night. I worry, it's not even October and it's too cold for him, but what can we do, he's not going to a home or a hospital, is he.'

I laughed in agreement.

'I'll come around after work,' I said, and the priest waved me on.

I was late again that evening, and Ignacio had gone to sleep again, and I had a strange thought that he was avoiding me somehow. I tried all week, and finally, on Monday, the day the café was closed, I went over there at noon, on a very pretty sunny, crisp autumn day. I walked, and admired the bright yellow glow coming off the row of gingko trees, and the oranges and browns of beeches and birches. The chestnuts were diseased, they were dying all over the city, and I was suddenly filled with the sadness of that autumn, that feeling of winter coming, and the thought that this might be the last time the chestnuts lost their leaves. Ignacio had died in the night, of course. The old bastard had avoided me, and slipped away in the dark. I went home again, and spent the day in bed, staring out at the sapphire blue sky and the streaks of planes coming and going. I consoled myself that I had tried, and perhaps I had known, and had wanted to say goodbye to the man who had been with me all of my life until that day.

Tuesday morning I went to the café, worked as usual. I took a tea break in the sunshine outside around two pm, it was getting cool already, and I saw a small cat. I was reminded of Ulrike. I took the day off and rode to the church, I intended to take her home with me. She would be fine in my apartment, it was on the second floor but my parents lived in the one below, with a small garden she could play in. I found her sitting on one of Ignacio's boxes. Father Elmer was in the front door, smoking, and he was relieved I was taking Ulrike. I dropped her off with my parents, where she jumped up onto my father's lap, delighting him. I thought I might as well go for a ride along the river.

On the way back past the church I saw there were people in Ignacio's yard, they were taking his things away, and piling them into a small van. I stopped to talk.

'Hello, where are you taking all that?' I asked the woman nearest me.

'Charity, trash, I don't know, we'll sort through it I guess. Robert?' she asked the man on the other side of the compound. He came over, the closed umbrella in his hand.

'All junk,' he said. I laughed.

'Do you know he once did this big heist, back in the sixties?' I asked. I have no idea why I would ask this stranger such a thing. The man looked at me intently for a moment.

'Come here,' he said, and I leaned my bike at the wall and went in to him.

'How do you know that?' he asked, and I felt a strange thrill, that feeling that I was going to suddenly know everything about the big mystery of my life, the only mystery of my life.

'He told me,' I said, 'years and years ago, when I was—fourteen, thirteen, I don't remember.'

The man laughed again. 'Yes, he was one of the famous Carnival heist six. They got away, the lot of them, and ten years ago, one of the women confessed.' I waited, I was holding my breath.

'According to her, poor Ignacio got nothing of value. He was the last one out, and all he got was a small box, that's what the woman told us.' I sighed. It made sense, of course, that Ignacio had nothing, poor old fool.

He lived in the church because he just did. There was nothing buried in the ground or hidden in a tree.

The man wasn't finished though. He was still laughing.

'The woman knew nothing about it. Ignacio got something. In fact, what he got was more valuable that anything those other idiots got. You're never going to guess. Go on, guess.'

I shook my head. I had no idea what this might be.

'Comics,' the man said. 'He had first edition comics, fifty of them. A million euros. At least.' He was still shaking his head and laughing as he walked away.

I thought I'd go for a long ride along the river, a very long ride. Maybe all the way to Rodenkirschen, and have a beer, before I rode home again. And then I'd read my forty-nine comic books again. And then I'd wake up the next morning and go to work, to the Clark Kent Café.

Acknowledgements

Thank you, Renuka, for trusting me with your wonderfully wicked concept. The endless ability of religion, this all too human invention, to turn people inside out with guilt, anger, hatred, and yes, sometimes love, is fascinating to me. Thank you also for your guidance, and meticulous reading and attention to detail while editing these stories.